SHELF LIFE

STORIES BY THE BOOK

SHELF LIFE

STORIES BY THE BOOK

EDITED BY

GARY PAULSEN

SIMON & SCHUSTER BOOKS FOR YOUNG READERS
New York   London   Toronto   Sydney   Singapore

SIMON & SCHUSTER BOOKS FOR YOUNG READERS
An imprint of SIMON & SCHUSTER CHILDREN'S PUBLISHING DIVISION
1230 Avenue of the Americas, New York, New York 10020

Compilation and introduction copyright © 2003 by Gary Paulsen
Foreword copyright © 2003 by Robert Wedgeworth
Introduction copyright © 2003 by Gary Paulsen
"Barcarole for Paper and Bones" copyright © 2003 by M. T. Anderson
"Clean Sweep" copyright © 2003 by Joan Bauer
"The Good Deed" copyright © 2003 by Marion Dane Bauer
"In Your Hat" copyright © 2003 by Ellen Conford
"Escape" copyright © 2003 by Margaret Peterson Haddix
"Follow the Water" copyright © 2003 by Jennifer L. Holm
"What's a Fellow to Do?" copyright © 2003 by Kathleen Karr
"Testing, Testing, 1 . . . 2 . . . 3" copyright © 2003 by A. LaFaye
"Tea Party Ends in Bloody Massacre, Film at 11" copyright © 2003 by Gregory Maguire
"Wet Hens" copyright © 2003 by Ellen Wittlinger

Book design by Interrobang Design Studio

The text for this book is set in Berthold Garamond.

Printed in the United States of America

2 4 6 8 10 9 7 5 3 1

Library of Congress Cataloging-in-Publication Data

Shelf life : stories by the book / Gary Paulsen.

p. cm.

Summary: Ten short stories in which the lives of young people in
different circumstances are changed by their encounters with books.

ISBN 0-689-84180-9

1. Children's stories, American. 2. Books and reading—Juvenile fiction.
[1. Books and reading—Fiction. 2. Short stories.] I. Paulsen, Gary.

PZ5 .S5185 2003

[Fic]—dc21

2002066901

FIRST
EDITION

To my friend Mike Printz,
whose life was devoted to putting books
in the hands of young readers

CONTENTS

CONTENTS

FOREWORD

Robert Wedgeworth, President, Proliteracy Worldwide

IN AN INCREASINGLY COMPLEX AND TECHNOLOGICAL SOCIETY, WHERE FIRST GRADERS WORK ON COMPUTERS AND YOU CAN TALK ONLINE TO SOMEONE ON THE OPPOsite side of the earth, it's hard to believe that there are adults in this country who can't read this sentence. It's hard to believe that more than forty million adults in the United States can't fill out a job application, follow directions on a prescription, access an ATM machine, or read a bedtime story to a child.

But it's true. In urban areas from New York City to Chicago and Houston to San Diego—and in small communities from Chipley, Florida, to College Station, Texas, to Ashtabula, Ohio—there are adults who lack literacy skills. They are men and women; white, African American, Asian American, and Latino; dropouts and high school graduates; born in the

United States and abroad. ProLiteracy Worldwide offers the key to unlock their potential—and to open the door to the whole world.

ProLiteracy Worldwide is an international, not-for-profit organization that provides local literacy services through a domestic network of more than 128,000 volunteers nationwide. In the United States the ProLiteracy network consists of more than 1,400 programs in fifty states in which professionally trained and managed volunteers tutor adults and their families. Our system provides tutoring, one-to-one or in small groups, at no charge to the student. Internationally, ProLiteracy supports seventy-nine partner programs in developing countries in Asia, Africa, the Middle East, and Latin America. ProLiteracy Worldwide was formed in 2002 from the merger of Literacy Volunteers of America, Inc., and Laubach Literacy International.

The 1993 National Adult Literacy Survey by the U.S. Department of Education showed that 21 to 23 percent of adults in this country function at the lowest level of literacy skills. ProLiteracy exists to reach and teach those individuals, and to enable them to achieve personal, educational, and job-related goals through literacy. ProLiteracy provides volunteer tutors with the professional training, materials, and support that enable them to provide this vital service to society.

Adult literacy students, many of whom may have learning disabilities, gain the skills that enable them to reach their goals as parents, employees, and citizens. Other adult literacy students are from countries all over the world, and enter into

ProLiteracy programs in order to gain English proficiency skills and become comfortable with life in the United States. ProLiteracy believes that the ability to read, write, and speak English well is the key to living a full and free life in America.

One of the more common reasons that adults seek to improve their literacy skills is a desire to serve as role models for their children. Parents want what is best for their children, including providing a supportive learning environment. Moreover, parents want to take advantage of opportunities for their own self-improvement and learning. Family literacy programs help them to achieve those goals and result in increased literacy skills, life skills, job skills, parenting skills, and self-esteem for parents as well as educational gains for children.

According to the 1996 National Assessment of Educational Progress, in homes where reading materials are plentiful, children have higher average reading proficiencies. The same study, involving 27,400 public and nonpublic school students, showed that children from homes where there are frequent discussions about school and reading had higher average proficiencies. ProLiteracy has a long-term commitment to family literacy services, enabling parents, caregivers, and children to enhance their skills together.

A variety of volunteer opportunities are available for people of all ages at ProLiteracy programs. Children and their parents can contact their local affiliates to find out how to help. ProLiteracy depends on its volunteer base to help it continue to provide assistance to adults with low-level literacy skills and to their families. In the same way, ProLiteracy depends on the support of those who, like Gary Paulsen, Simon & Schuster, and the authors featured in this anthology, believe in the value of adult literacy. ProLiteracy deeply appreciates their commitment to adults working to increase their literacy skills.

SHELF LIFE

LIFE

STORIES BY THE BOOK

INTRODUCTION

―――――――――――――

Gary Paulsen

$\mathcal{B}$OOKS SAVED MY LIFE.

First reading them, then writing them.

As surely as my lead dog Cookie pulled me from the bottom of a lake after I fell through the ice, books are the reason I survived my miserable childhood. As certainly as my sloop Scallywag has safely taken me through storms and huge seas, books have sustained me as an adult.

The awfulness of my childhood has been well covered. But I remember two women who took the time to help me when I was a boy and both women, not so coincidentally, helped me with books.

Because I lived from the age of seven to when I was nearly ten in the Philippine Islands and had a private military tutor, I had never been to a public school.

We came back to the States when I was just short of ten and moved to Washington, D.C., so my father, who was in the army, could work at the Pentagon. My mother promptly enrolled me in public school, took me there the first morning, handed me over to a teacher, and left.

I was painfully shy, terrified at the mob of kids and could not go into the room. It was an old school and at the back of the classroom, there was a cloakroom, a shallow closet the width of the room but closed in except for one door. I went in the closet and took my coat off with the rest of the children but then I could not leave, simply could not make my legs move to walk out into the classroom. I was too frightened.

There were many things the teacher could have done wrong. She could have forced me out, dragged me into the classroom, could have made me leave. Instead she did everything right.

She looked into the closet, saw me sitting back in the corner and disappeared for a moment and said something to the children. Then she came back into the closet and sat down next to me in the corner and put her arm around me.

She had a book, a picture book. I cannot recall the contents of the book except that it had a horse's head on the cover and she sat next to me quietly for a time and read to me softly and let me turn the pages. I was lost in the quiet of the cloakroom, lost in the book so deeply that everything else fell away.

After a time, it could have been ten minutes or an hour or my whole life, she asked me if I thought I could come out into the room and take my seat at a desk. I nodded and she stood and took my hand and led me into the classroom.

A few years later, when I was thirteen, another woman, a librarian, gave me another book and I consider every good thing that has ever happened to me since then a result of that woman handing me that book.

I'd been wandering the streets of the small Minnesota town we lived in one bitter winter evening, waiting for the drunks in the bars to get juiced. I sold newspapers, trying to scrape together a little money so that I could buy better clothes, believing, as kids do, that the right clothes might somehow lift me from my wretchedly unpopular social life. And if I waited for the men who hung around in the bars to get a few drinks in them, I could hustle them for extra change.

I stopped in the library to warm up. The librarian noticed me, called me over, and asked if I wanted a library card. Then she handed me a card with my name on it and gave me a book.

Later that night back at home, or what passed for home—a crummy apartment in the bad part of town—I took the book, a box of crackers, and a jar of grape jelly down to the basement, to a hideaway I'd created behind the furnace where someone had abandoned a creaky old armchair under a bare lightbulb.

I sat in the corner, eating jelly-smeared crackers, plodding through the book. It took me forever to read. I was such a poor reader that, by the time I'd finished a page, I'd have forgotten what I'd read on the page before and I'd have to go back. That first book must have taken me over a month to finish, hunched over the pages late at night.

I wish I could remember the name of that first book—I can't even remember what it was about. What I do remember about that evening at the library was that it marked the first of many nights the librarian would give me a book. "Here," she'd say, handing me a few battered volumes. "I think you'll like these." She would hand select books that she thought would interest me—Westerns, mysteries, survival tales, science fiction, Edgar Rice Burroughs. I would take them home to hide in the basement and read; I'd bring them back and we'd talk about them, and she'd give me more books.

But she wasn't just giving me books, she was giving me . . . everything. She gave me the first hint I'd ever had in my entire life that there was something other than my drunken parents screaming at each other in the kitchen. She handed me a world where I wasn't going to get beaten up by the school bullies. She showed me places where it didn't hurt all the time.

I read terribly at first but as I did more of it, the books became more a part of me and within a short time they gave me a life, a look at life outside myself that made me look forward instead of backward.

Years later, after I'd graduated from high school, joined the army, gotten married, had children, and made a career as an electronics engineer working in satellite tracking, books once again changed the course of my life. This time, though, I wrote them.

I was sitting in a satellite tracking station at about nine

o'clock at night when suddenly I knew that I had to be a writer. In that instant, I gave up or lost everything that had made up my life until that point—my work, my family, certainly my earning potential.

Writing had suddenly become everything . . . everything . . . to me.

I stood up from the console, handed in my security badge, and headed for Hollywood. I had to go to a place where I knew writers were; I had to be near them, had to learn from them. I got a job as a proofreader of a men's magazine, going from earning $500 a week to $400 a month, and apprenticed myself to a couple of editors.

These two men gave me writing assignments, and in order to continue receiving their help, I had to write an article, a chapter of a book, or a short story every night, every single night, no exceptions, no excuses, for them to critique. If I missed a single day, they would no longer help me.

I have been writing for over thirty years, spent most of it starving, trying to make it work for me, in my mind; trying to make words come together in the right patterns, movements, what some have called the loops and whorls of the story dance, and it has always been hard. It is, sometimes, still difficult. But I love writing more now, I think, than I ever have. The way the stories dance, the rhythms and movements of them, is grandly exciting to me.

I remember the first acceptance letter, the first time a publisher told me my writing was worthy of publication, the first after many, many rejections. There will never be another first like this one; not first love nor first hope nor first time never, no never like this.

Dear author: We have decided to publish your book.

Can you imagine? Your life, your work, your hopes and thoughts and songs and breath, we have decided to publish your book. We have decided to publish you. Such words thunder, burn into your mind, your soul.

Since then I have written every day and I have told many stories. Stories of love and death and cold and heat and ice and flame, stories sad and stories happy and stories of laughter and tears and places soft and hard, of dogs and the white-blink of arctic ice, stories of great men and beautiful women and souls and devils and gods, stories of lost dreams and found joys and aches and torture and great rolling hills and towering storms and things quick and hot and slow and dull, stories of graves and horses, pigs and kings, war and the times between wars, stories of children's cheeks and the soft hair at a woman's temple when it is moist, stories of rage and spirit and spit and blood and bodies on fences and hay so sweet you could eat the grass.

I write from my life, from what I see and hear and smell and feel, from personal inspection at zero altitude and I write because it is, simply, all that I am, because in the end I do not want to do any other thing as much as I want to write. But the force behind it, the thing that pushes me to write, that wakes me at night with story ideas, that makes the hair on the back of my neck go up when a story works, that causes my breath to stop and hold with a sentence that comes right, and that makes coming to the computer or the pad of paper every morning with a cup of tea and a feeling of wonderful newness and expectations, the engine that drives me to write is, surely, love.

I personally want just two things. I want to write, and I want as many young readers as possible to see what I write. That's it. To write and to have readers.

I work all the time. I get up at four thirty in the morning, meditate for half an hour, then start working. Not always writing, but working. If I'm not writing, I read and study and write until I fall asleep at night.

I owe everything I am and everything that I will ever be to books.

The stories in this collection range from fantasy to farce, from realism to science fiction, but they all have something in common: books that change lives.

Ellen Conford's "In Your Hat" introduces a practical joker who gets his comeuppance when the girl of his dreams decides to help him with his book report.

In "Escape," by Margaret Peterson Haddix, a chance encounter with one of the volunteers at the homeless shelter where Isabel has been living with her mother makes Isabel consider that there might be a reason why her mother spends so much money on trashy novels.

In Jennifer L. Holm's "Follow the Water," a girl who never wanted to go to Mars with her scientist parents in the first place has to make the hardest decision she's ever faced, just when things seem like they might start to get better.

"Testing, Testing, 1 . . . 2 . . . 3," by A. LaFaye, shows a boy who is falling behind in school until he finally gets to learn things his own way, thanks to a magic book that the mysterious woman next door gives him.

In "Tea Party Ends in Bloody Massacre, Film at 11," by Gregory Maguire, a decidedly unladylike girl wins over her mother's stuffy visitors with the help of a book—even if the story she tells has nothing to do with the book she's holding.

The hero of Kathleen Karr's "What's a Fellow to Do?" is a young pickpocket who plans to make a fortune at the 1893 Columbian Exposition of Chicago. What he ends up finding there, however—an abandoned baby, just like baby Moses in the Bible—might just turn his life around.

"Wet Hens," by Ellen Wittlinger, tells how a favorite childhood book creates a bond between two girls when one of them gets into a fight with her best friend.

In Marion Dane Bauer's "The Good Deed," Heather's volunteer assignment—to read to a blind woman all summer—seems like a job to do, until the girl across the hall makes Heather realize that helping people is more than just a matter of duty.

"Barcarole for Paper and Bones," by M. T. Anderson, is an intricate puzzle of a story: a mysteriously deserted ship makes those who find it hope that the ship's written records will make some sense of the situation—but in fact, just the opposite proves true.

In Joan Bauer's "Clean Sweep," a girl and her brother unearth a book from a bitter old woman's childhood when they clean out her attic, which leads the woman to reconnect with a sister she hasn't spoken to in years.

It was and still is a wonder for me, what books are and how they become part of a reader's mind and soul. I thank all of the writers I've read and all of the readers who've read my books for allowing me the unending thrill of being a part of this crazy dance of words. And I wish the same kind of joy for everyone who holds a copy of this book in their hands.

Sales of this book benefit ProLiteracy Worldwide, an international network with more than 1,400 programs based in the United States and 79 partner programs abroad, whose mission is to change lives through literacy.

IN YOUR HAT

—⁐———————⁐—

Ellen Conford

I WAS IN THE NONSILENT STUDY AREA OF THE LIBRARY ON THE LAST SUNDAY OF MIDWINTER BREAK WHEN ARIEL GREENBANKS NOTICED ME.

I'd been trying to get Ariel Greenbanks to notice me for almost two years now, and the results had been grim to none. So when she paused next to my chair that afternoon, I seized the opportunity.

"Hey, good lookin'," I said. "Come here often?"

"As a matter of fact, yes." She picked up a couple of the books littering the table in front of me.

"Joseph Conrad?" she said. "Jane Austen?"

"Well, uh—"

I hesitated. She was seeing a side of me she'd never seen before, which wasn't surprising, since I don't have that side.

Apparently she liked the Mensa type. That was probably why my great sense of humor and my legendary reputation for practical jokes had never attracted her. Well, that and maybe the handcuffs.

But you can't base a relationship on lies, I told myself. It would be dishonest. I couldn't pretend I was an intellectual giant. At least, not for more than eleven minutes.

"Actually," I began, "I'm kind of in a crisis here."

"What kind of crisis?" Ariel asked.

"An emergency book report," I told her.

"Oh. When is it due?"

"Tomorrow."

She raised her eyebrows. "Tomorrow," she repeated. "That *is* an emergency."

"Yup." I sighed deeply.

"Well, which one of these did you read?" she asked.

"I haven't exactly gotten to the reading stage yet," I admitted. I didn't want to tell her that I had only gotten to the "which is the shortest book you can find?" stage.

"Wow." She looked up at the clock over the reference desk. "Dennis," she said, "you are in big trouble."

"I know, I know." And yet . . .

Ariel Greenbanks was talking to me! Ariel Greenbanks cared about my emergency. Ariel Greenbanks was wearing a cute pink sweater and smelled like carnations.

Suddenly all my troubles seemed so far away.

She slid into the chair next to mine. She scooped some of the books toward her, and started examining the titles.

She wanted to help me! I didn't move. I could hardly breathe. I was afraid I was imagining all this, and that any moment she would disappear. So I just sat there and breathed in the carnation scent, and let my eyes rest on the pinkness that was Ariel.

"All of these are pretty short," she said.

"Yeah, short was the first requirement," I answered. "Short, and with big print."

Her eyes narrowed. She frowned.

"I mean, because of the crisis," I explained quickly. "If I didn't have to hand in the report tomorrow . . . I mean, it's not like I don't like to read."

"Maybe you could write about something you've already read," Ariel suggested. "What was the last book you liked?"

"The Sponge People of Cyberia."

Ariel nodded. "I see what you mean. Not a book report book."

"Mr. Frazetti has this blind prejudice against science fiction," I complained. "I don't understand it."

"Okay, have you read anything that isn't science fiction?" she asked.

"The Microbe Hunters," I said. "But I can't use that one."

"Why not?" she asked.

"Well, the thing is . . ." I decided that now was not the time to explain. Why tell Ariel that after four years of handing in the same book report that I'd written in seventh grade, the book report cops had finally caught up with me?

Frankly, I don't think teachers ought to be allowed to trade information about their students with other teachers. Isn't that like a breach of doctor-patient confidentiality?

But why go into that now? Now, when Ariel was finally noticing me? I mean, in a good way. Not like with the lab rat.

Some day, maybe after the birth of our first child, I'd tell her the story behind *The Microbe Hunters*. We'd laugh about it together. "Oh, Dennis," she'd say, cuddling our baby. "You're so bad! But in a good way."

Suddenly the library lights blinked on and off. I looked around, dazed.

"It's closing time," Ariel said.

Reality finally smacked me in the face. "What am I going to do?" I started snatching up the books on the table, looking at the titles, tossing them aside. A couple of them landed on the floor. I tried to load a bunch under my arm.

I looked desperately at Ariel. I must have resembled a puppy pleading to be rescued from the pound.

Because she smiled. Gently. Sympathetically.

"You'd better come to my house," she said.

Her house. I was walking to her house. Then I was in her house. With *her*. I was dreaming. I wasn't dreaming.

Her parents were in the family room watching something athletic on television.

"We'll work in my room," Ariel said.

And there I was at last. In Ariel's room. Alone with Ariel. She and I. Her and me? Whatever.

She'd been quiet on the walk from the library. She'd said she was trying to think of a book that would be good for my report.

"And short," I reminded her. "It's got to be short."

Now, as I looked around her room, she walked over to a bookcase under her window. She bent down and started scanning the titles. I sank into the chair next to her desk and scanned Ariel.

"Darn it," she said. "I can't find it." She straightened up and turned around. "It was perfect," she said. "Short, but a minor classic. Mr. Frazetti would really have been impressed."

"Well, um–" I tilted my head toward her computer. "Did you save your report? Maybe I could . . . you know. . . ."

"I didn't read it for an assignment," Ariel said. "Just for fun. Oh, it was so great! It was about the millinery industry in France and this poor little woman who had all her hat designs stolen by an evil corporation. And then–"

"You read this for fun?" Much as I wanted to wow Ariel with my intellectualness, I couldn't help it.

"Honestly, it was really good," she insisted. "And so vivid, so alive! I mean, you could smell the slop in the Paris streets. You could feel the hunger and the cold gnawing at you."

"Uh, right," I said. "I know what you mean."

"And it's so relevant," she went on. "Even now. You could compare it to how today's giant corporations swallow up the little guy."

She sighed. "But, I can't find it. *C'est la vie.*"

"*La vie,*" I repeated. Even in times of crisis, my sense of humor doesn't desert me.

I thought I saw a brief scowl flash across her brow. I hoped she hadn't suddenly remembered the twenty-six pizzas I'd had delivered to her.

"I really shouldn't do this," she began slowly. "But it *is* an emergency."

"What shouldn't you do?" I asked eagerly. "And will you do it?"

"I could tell you about the book," Ariel said. "I mean, I really shouldn't, but . . ."

"Oh, Ariel, would you do that? For me?"

I couldn't believe it. Had she finally realized that we were destined to be together? Had she seen beyond the jokes and snappy patter, and discovered the tormented soul beneath? The Me who longed for her, but who could only express his love behind a mask of comedy?

She perched on the edge of her bookcase. "Can you stay awhile?" she asked. "This will take some time."

"I have time," I said. I don't think my voice cracked too noticeably.

I went home with five pages of notes that Ariel had dictated. I scarfed down supper without tasting it, and headed for my computer.

It wasn't easy to concentrate on my book report with visions of Ariel dancing in my head. I kept seeing her in her soft, pink sweater, when I was supposed to be thinking of French hats. I kept hearing her clear, sweet voice while I was supposed to be imagining the crude, clashing noises of the Parisian slums.

But it really was a good story, and after a while, I got caught up in my own description of it.

This poor but honest French country girl marries a real loser who gets drunk a lot and beats her, and finally dies when he gets run over by a thresher in the potato fields where he's been trying to eke out a living by growing (of course) potatoes.

She goes to Paris to try and support herself by making hats, which she'd always wanted to do ever since she saw a tattered copy of *Elle* magazine when she was a child.

Well, it turns out she's really talented, and all the Paris society ladies start coming to buy their hats from her. Things are looking up at last for Madame de Maupassant.

Until she meets this slick, high-class society guy (named Guy, as a matter of fact). Only, he's been down on his luck too, and really needs money to pay off his gambling debts.

But Madame de Maupassant doesn't know any of that. She falls madly in love with him, and he asks her to marry him. *Happiness at last!* she thinks.

But on the day they're supposed to be married, Guy disappears, taking all her original hat designs with him. He sells her designs to Le Chic Chapeau, a big hat company, so he can pay off his debts, and then runs off to Algeria and is never heard from again.

Madame de Maupassant is heartbroken and gets tuberculosis, and wastes away to a pitiful shadow of her former self. She doesn't even have the money for a bowl of soup, let alone medicine.

Finally, just as she takes her last dying breath, there's a knock on the door of her attic room. It's one of her old customers, who wants her to design all the hats for her daughter's wedding.

But it's too late. Madame de Maupassant can barely whisper, "*Entrez*" when she gasps and dies.

I'm telling you, it was a terrific story. I could understand why Ariel was so moved by it. I felt myself almost sniffling a little as I wrote out the plot.

I did what Ariel had suggested, and made a comparison between *Madame de Maupassant* and the economics of today. I wrote how the book was still relevant and meaningful, even though it was written a hundred and twenty years ago.

I spell-checked, then printed out my report, and was asleep before midnight . . . to dream of Ariel, in pink, trying on hats. Big, flowery, poufy, old-fashioned hats. And asking me which one I liked best.

"But of course I care what you think, Dennis," she said. "I want to look pretty for you."

On Monday I handed in my book report to Mr. Frazetti. "It's not on *The Microbe Hunters*," I told him.

He gave me a fake shocked look. "You mean, you read another book?"

I spent the next two days trying to thank Ariel.

I wanted to buy her lunch on Tuesday, but she pointed to the tray in front of her. "I have lunch already," she said.

On Wednesday I asked her if she'd go to the library with

me. I had this sudden urge to read another book by Emile Bovary. Actually, I had an urge to read _Madame de Maupassant._ Ariel had made it sound so good.

Plus, in case Mr. Frazetti asked me any questions about it—like if, for some reason he didn't believe I'd really read such a famous classic—I'd be ready for him.

But Ariel couldn't go to the library Wednesday afternoon. She said she had band practice.

On Thursday, Mr. Frazetti handed our book reports back. I sat straight and proud at my desk, waiting for my A to reach me, picturing the kiss of congratulations Ariel would give me when I showed her my report.

Mr. Frazetti walked slowly up and down between the rows of desks, taking forever to give back our papers. Usually I was in no hurry to get my assignments back. But today was different.

I heard groans, and deep sighs, and an occasional cheerful yip! as the other kids got their book reports returned.

Finally Mr. Frazetti stood at my desk. He thrust the report at me. "_Really,_ Mr. Murphy," he said.

That was all. "_Really,_ Mr. Murphy." He moved on to Oliver Cohen, who screamed when he saw his grade.

I looked down at my paper.

"Madame de Maupassant, by Emile Bovary."

"F!!" Mr. Frazetti had scrawled across the top. Just like that—with two exclamation points. Underneath, he'd written, "F as in FAKE!! Do you think I'm an idiot??"

I couldn't have been more stunned if I'd been captured by the Sponge People of Cyberia.

What did he mean? What was fake? How could he possibly know that I hadn't really read the book? How could he know that Ariel had told me the story?

Had she made a mistake in the details? Did she get the plot wrong?

I leafed through the paper to the last page. At the bottom Mr. Frazetti had written: "There will be no Makeup for this assignment. You have made up enough already."

I put my hand over my eyes. Despair and confusion overwhelmed me. Just as Le Chic Chapeau had overwhelmed Madame de Maupassant.

I cornered Ariel at the stop sign near the parking lot exit. She was with two other girls, who started giggling the moment they saw me.

I pulled out my book report. "Look at this! *Look* at this!"

She glanced at the paper. "Oh, my," she said. "An F. That's not good."

"Not good?" I repeated. "It's terrible! Why did I get an F?"

"Well," she began, "maybe because I made it up."

"Made it up?" I repeated stupidly. "Made what up?"

"The book," she said.

"What are you *talking* about?"

She smiled, a sweet, devious smile. "The thing is," she said, "there really is no such book as *Madame de Maupassant.*"

"No such book?" My head felt like it was going to explode.

"No," she said. "No such book. I made it up. The whole story."

"But—but—" I couldn't stop stammering. I couldn't stop gaping at her. I couldn't stop her friends from laughing at me.

"But *why?*" I wailed.

"It was a joke, Dennis," she said sweetly. "Just a little joke."

She started to walk away, with her friends on either side of her still giggling.

"It's not funny!" I yelled. "Ariel, that was not a funny joke!"

She turned, and tilted her (beautiful, golden blond) head to one side. "You don't think so?"

"No!" I shouted. "I don't think so! You really got me in trouble!"

She put her hands on her hips, and shook her head. "For heaven's sake, Dennis," she said. "What's happened to your sense of humor?"

Then she turned, and walked off down the street.

ESCAPE

—◦————————————◦—

Margaret Peterson Haddix

MAMA'S BUYING ANOTHER BOOK TO SEND TO DADDY IN PRISON.

"Think he'd like this one?" she asks, pointing. The cover of the book shows a girl falling out of her dress, top first. A big muscle-man-type stands above her, looking squinty-eyed and mean. Like, *I'll protect you. Won't let nobody but me look at your breasts.*

I look at the floor.

"Thought he was learning Spanish," I mumble.

"I already sent him them books," Mama says. "'Sides, he's gotta take a break some time from studying."

I bet he takes breaks, all right. He's in prison.

But you can't tell Mama stuff like that. I shrug, like I'm giving Mama permission to buy the romance book. I shuffle up to the counter with her.

We're in the bookstore on Main Street, the only one you can get to without a car. The better stores are at the mall, way out, just about in the country. But that's okay. Might be someone I know hanging out at the mall. Here, nobody'll hear what Mama's going to say next.

"You'll have to mail it for me," she tells the clerk. "Prison won't take packages unless they're straight from the store."

I stare at a rack of paperbacks like I really care what's selling best. I pretend I'm not with Mama. Mama knows. Oh, Mama knows.

"You've got no call, being ashamed of your daddy in prison," she's told me more than once. "Ain't your fault. Nobody can hold it against you."

Sometimes, Mama doesn't sit in the same room with reality.

No—make that most of the time. She turns around, hollers at me, "What time is it, Isabel? We got a few minutes 'fore we gotta catch that bus to the shelter?"

I hide behind the rack of books, but it's too late. The clerk's already seen me. He's one of those mousy men—thick glasses, thin hair. He gives me a little half smile of pity that digs in worse than Mama's words. It'd be better if he was one of those that squint their nasty little eyes at me, just waiting to catch me shoplifting. Them I can glare back at.

Mama uses her last ten to pay. I follow her out to the sidewalk.

"It's not a shelter," I say when I catch up with her. "It's a church."

"Same thing," she says. "We're using it like a shelter."

It doesn't bother Mama that Daddy's in prison. She doesn't care that we got kicked out of our apartment back in May, the day before my eighth-grade graduation.

I didn't go to my eighth-grade graduation. We spent that day touring social service agencies, asking for a new home. It never occurred to me we wouldn't be getting one. Never thought I'd be adding "less" to that word. Home. Less. Homeless.

Once you're homeless, nobody wants you. City won't even let anybody build new homeless shelters. So they bus us around to different churches, a new one every week. We sleep in Sunday school rooms with pictures of Jesus and lambs on the walls, kindergarten craft projects where everything's glued crooked. Makes me itch, wanting to put all the popsicle sticks straight, line up all the lambies' faces.

Mama's supposed to be getting her act together. Supposed to be making a plan. That's what all the social workers tell her.

"Anyone else, I'd be losing patience with," I heard one of them tell her this morning. "But I *like* you, Evvie. You've got a great attitude. You don't let things get you down. You've just got to take a little more responsibility for your life."

Mama skipped her job training class this afternoon, came and got me early from summer school, just so we could go spend her last ten on a trashy romance book for Daddy in prison.

Oh, yeah. That's responsibility.

• • •

This week's church is Presbyterian, which means they don't try to cram any religion down our throats. They do seem awful eager to make sure we get enough potato chips with our hamburgers at dinner.

"Can I interest you in a refill, missy?" one of the men says, roaming the aisle between our fold-up chairs with a big bag of Ruffles. "Can't have you going hungry, now."

He's got a face like rubber. Seems like the corners of his mouth could never sag down into anything less than a full grin.

"No, thanks," I mutter.

The workers retreat into the kitchen and eat their dinners there, standing at the counters. They're all talking together. Laughing.

Sometimes I wonder what those workers are like when they're not with us, being cheerful to keep up our spirits. Does rubber-face ever fight with his wife? Does he ever get up in the morning and stare in the mirror and feel bad about who he is? Does he ever yell at his kids? Do his kids ever yell at him?

Dinner's over. Mama takes her plate and my plate up to the counter, and the workers give her big smiles, like they're rewarding a dog for doing a new trick.

"The child-care volunteers are here," rubber-face announces.

Women come in and take toddlers' sticky hands, start to lead them away. "Ooh, let's wash you off first," one of the women says to a little girl. "You wouldn't want to get catsup on any of the toys, would you?"

It wouldn't be so bad being a little kid here. You wouldn't know you were homeless. You'd have all sorts of people feeding you and oohing and aahing over you. And child care looks kind of fun. They've got a toy kitchen down in the playroom. I can remember wanting one of those real bad when I was four. But Mama was spending all her extra money on sending books to Daddy in prison, even back then.

The little kids are gone, and now it's real quiet in the dining room. It's just me and the grown-ups left.

That's another thing about being homeless. I've got nowhere to go in the evenings. I'm too old for child care, but I'm too young for all the classes they make the grown-ups take. "Making Good Choices." "Balancing a Budget." "Preparing for a Job Interview."

Bet I already know more about any of that stuff than Mama does.

"What you going to do, baby?" she says, putting her arm around my shoulder and squeezing.

I want to get out of this church, maybe take a walk. They've let me do that at some of the other churches. But the workers here don't like it.

"It's going to be dark soon," one of them said when he stopped me the first night. "This isn't the greatest neighborhood. It's no place for a young girl to be wandering around alone at night."

I could have argued. Darkness was hours away. And the neighborhood around the church is a billion times better than where Mama and I live. Used to live. But there was something in his face—some fear of what I might do—that made me keep my mouth shut.

"Guess I'll go on down to the youth room," I tell Mama now.

The youth room is down the hall. It has a pool table and a Ping-Pong table and a bunch of stupid boxed-up games like Chinese checkers and Trivial Pursuit. None of those are things I can play alone. But Mama doesn't seem to remember that. She gives my shoulder another squeeze and releases me.

I look in at the window of the playroom where all the little kids are. A wild-haired doll is flying through the air because some of the boys are using it like a football. One little girl, Keisha something, is sitting in the corner crying.

I could go in and help. I could play with the toy kitchen and pretend I was just doing it for the little kids' sake, getting them involved. But I walk on. I turn the corner toward the youth room. It'll be nice to have the whole place all to myself. There's nothing I have all to myself anymore.

The light's already on in the youth room, but I don't think anything of that at first. I shut the door behind me and let out a deep breath. Alone. Finally. Suddenly it seems like I've been holding my breath ever since rubber-face served me dinner. No, since we were at the bookstore. No, since we were evicted.

Only maybe it started before that. I'd say I haven't gotten enough air since the first time Daddy got sent to prison, but I don't remember that. I barely remember Daddy.

I close my eyes, breathing in and out. Maybe I sway. I sure don't see the girl on the couch.

"I bugged out, too," she says.

My eyes spring open. My mouth does too. I jerk my head around, looking for the source of the voice.

"Oops, sorry. Didn't mean to scare you," the girl says.

I shrug, recovering. Trapping my breath again, I guess. Putting on my careful face. I look this girl over real good. She's curled up on the couch as cozy as a cat. Two things strike me all at once.

First, she's one of the worker volunteers, and seems to think I am too. Well, I could be, I guess. We're dressed the same: jean shorts, tank tops, hair pulled back in ponytails.

Second, she's got her finger stuck in the middle of a fat paperback. And I recognize it. She's reading the same book Mama just finished sending Daddy in prison.

"My parents dragged me down here," the girl says. "They actually thought I was going to help. 'If you're too shy to interact directly with the people, you can dish up food in the kitchen,' my dad kept saying. Yeah, right. My bet is, those people don't even want us helping them."

I'm guessing this girl's dad is rubber-face. Just the way she does the imitation.

"Don't you hate how parents are always trying to make you a better person?" the girl says.

I think, *no*. I can't think of one single time my mama ever tried to make me a better person. She never gives me the drugs lecture, about how I should stay away from them because that's what landed my daddy in prison. She never makes me go to school when I say I don't feel so great, even though she's got to know I'm faking those stomachaches. She's never even been too big on making me brush my teeth before bed.

Only thing my mama's ever forced me to do was go with her to buy books for Daddy in prison.

Something strange happens next. My body feels all jangly all of a sudden, like I've been sound asleep and some big noise just jolted me awake. And I'm lying there in the dark with my nerves jumping, trying to figure out what the noise was.

"What are you reading?" I say carefully.

The girl turns the book over in her hand, looks at the cover like she's forgotten what it is.

"Escapist drivel," she says, sighing. "Just something to make me feel like I'm not here."

She acts like I'm going to understand those big words. Escapist drivel. But suddenly I kind of do. Escapist. Escape.

Just something to make me feel like I'm not here.

I have chills all of a sudden, and I know I'm not getting sick.

"If you knew someone in prison," I say slowly, "and you was going to send them a package—what would you send them?"

I'm sure I've given away that I'm not one of the volunteers, that this church is the closest thing I've got to a home. That I know someone in prison. But I don't care. The girl doesn't act like she notices.

"Is that one of those brainteaser questions?" she asks. "Okay, I'll bite. Let's see, prison. Aren't you supposed to send people cakes with axes or guns or something like that baked into them, so the prisoner can escape? Except maybe that'd be a bad thing, because then if the person got caught trying to escape, he'd probably be shot or killed or something. So—"

I can't wait for this girl to think everything through.

"Would you send that book?" I break in. I point at the book in her hand.

The girl looks down at the book again, kind of studies the cover. The colors are so bright they almost hurt my eyes.

"I guess," she says finally. "Sure. Let the person feel like they're on a tropical island for a few hours—and in *love* instead of in prison."

She grins like it's all a joke. But I feel like I've got fireworks going off inside my head. And with each blast, I see something new.

I never once asked Mama why she sends Daddy books in prison. I never once asked if he reads them. Maybe he doesn't. Maybe he does.

Mama doesn't read much, herself. She can't, much. But those books she sends Daddy—that's her way of sending him an escape that's not drugs or drinking or a gun in a cake. The romance books are her love letters. The textbooks are her hopes: *You gonna be a better person when you get out.*

"You can be in love and in prison, all at the same time," I tell this girl.

"Okay," she says, backing off. "I don't know much about prison." Like she's apologizing.

I've scared her, acting fierce. All at once, I feel sorry for this girl, a little chicken tourist from the suburbs. Someone who thinks *she* needs an escape.

But maybe she does. How would I know?

I look around the youth room, and it seems like a different place, and I'm a different person in it. The posterboard hanging crooked, with the words "Jesus loves you" packed in too tight because whoever wrote it ran out of room—that doesn't bother me anymore. The pool balls lying quiet on the green felt don't make me want to grab one and hurl it at the wall anymore.

I can be Mama's daughter and believe in the power of escapist drivel, and that doesn't mean I'm going to live in a homeless shelter all my life.

I can have a daddy in prison, and care about him, and that doesn't mean I'll ever be sent to prison myself.

"Hey," the girl says. "You want to borrow this book? It's not really that good, but, I don't know. You might want to read it. You can just leave it somewhere here when you're done."

I look over and she's holding out the book to me, helping someone in spite of herself.

I take the book from her.

"Yeah," I say. "Thanks."

FOLLOW THE WATER

Jennifer L. Holm

I'M FLOATING IN WATER.

Next to me, Nana is bobbing on her back, looking up at the same blue sky, her white hair tied in a thick braid. She is wearing her lifeguard-red bathing suit, and her arms trail in the water at her sides in smooth, unhurried motions. Seagulls scream above our heads, swooping low, diving across the waves as if trying to get our attention, but it doesn't bother us. It is so peaceful out here, so perfect.

We are just two mermaids enjoying the freedom of the waves, the tug of the undertow, the rush of water all around us, part of the ocean itself.

"Georgie," Nana says, her voice smiling with pleasure. "It's heaven to be here with you."

And then a wave comes up from behind, crashes over us, and I wake up, breathing in stale musty air.

And realize I'm still on Mars.

"Ouch!" I say.

The doctor pats my arm. "Hmm, sorry about that. I'm having a hard time finding a vein."

"Can we do this another day?" I plead. "Look at my arm!" It is covered with bruises.

"Georgiana," my mother says, shaking her head. "Come on, don't be silly."

Easy for her to say. She's not the one who's getting stuck with a needle.

"It's very important for us to gather biological data for future colonists," she adds as if this will somehow make this fun.

See, my mother's a scientist. Actually, she's a geologist like my father and they live for experiments and collecting data. My parents love Mars, which kind of makes sense, I guess, since Mars is really just a big rock. They spend hours talking about geological formations and whether the Holden Crater was once a lake. But when it comes to anything involving people or feelings she doesn't have a clue.

"I'm sick of this," I say, reluctantly baring my arm for the doctor. "I feel like a lab rat."

The doctor shrugs at me apologetically. "We have to keep an eye on you. We still don't know how the lower gravity will affect your development."

I've heard this about a million times. I'm not even supposed to be here. Only adults over eighteen are allowed to go to Mars but they let me come because they thought I'd finished puberty. Mars gravity is one-third of Earth's and I guess they want to avoid turning us into mutants. Although I suppose I could tell them a thing or two about their mutant theory of gravity. See, I've grown four inches in the time I've been here. Not that I'm complaining. I was kind of on the short side before anyway.

We are the fourth wave of pioneers, known as Fourths. The second wave erected the medical cabin I am standing in. It's thick black plastic, sturdy enough to protect us from the solar UV radiation, which could kill you, give you terrible skin cancer. That's what the Firsts found out. Some of them came back and had to have their noses removed. Pretty gross, if you ask me. Now the whole compound is a rabbit's warren of connecting plastic tunnels.

I guess there's nothing like a little death and disaster to make you figure out how to do things right. But all those unmanned robots that explored the planet seemed pretty good. They transmitted back maps, and geological findings, and climate information. So that by the time the first fifty people and one dog were sent to Mars, they thought they knew the score.

But, I mean, I suppose it's not easy to organize the pesky little business of living on a deserted rock in the middle of space. There's the crazy weather, and the subzero freezing cold, and the dust storms, and the little fact that it takes six months to get here packed on a shuttle like a bunch of sardines. In my opinion, there's a pretty good reason that Mars is uninhabited, but why would anyone listen to a fourteen-year-old?

The doctor jabs the needle in my arm again. It stings and I wince.

"There we go," he says. "Just relax."

I watch as a tube of dark red blood is sucked out. The doctor yanks the needle out, slaps on a Band-Aid, and as I rub my arm, I can't help but wonder if they sent this guy to Mars to get him off Earth. Talk about bedside manner.

"There. That wasn't so bad, now was it?" my mother says brightly.

"Whoops," the doctor says. "I need one more tube."

"No more blood," I say.

I put up with a lot on this planet. Like no friends, and rehydrated food, and having to perform like a pony on transmissions for kids back home, but enough is enough.

"Georgiana," my mother says, looking at the doctor.

"No more!" I run to the door, and then freeze. Because on this dumb planet I can't even make a dramatic exit.

I have to put on my stupid survival suit first.

I flip open the flap and head down the plastic hallway. It's eerily quiet, the way it always gets before a bad dust storm hits, and I shiver a little.

It's cold on Mars, colder than you can even imagine. The average temperature here is negative eighty-one degrees, and believe me, that's pretty darn cold when you have to go to the bathroom in the middle of the night.

On the trip here, I read a book called *Red Mars,* by this guy Kim Stanley Robinson. It's this famous science fiction book written a long time ago about what Mars might be like for the first colonists. In it, the Mars colonists live a pretty comfortable life in these beautiful domed cities that have amazing views of the surrounding landscape. He made it sound not half bad, actually. And then I got here.

Which is why I guess it's called science fiction and not reality.

But Mr. Robinson did get the part about the dust right. See, the dust on Mars is so superfine, so microscopic, that it blows right through all the plastic tents we live in. The plastic keeps the air in and the UV rays out, but not the dust. I don't know why. And it's everywhere. In your eyes, in your ears, in your hair. Even your belly button. Most of the people who live here seem to get used to it, but not me. I mean, how do you get used to finding dust up your nose every morning? Not to mention, it's impossible to get the taste of it out of your mouth, rusty, like you're losing a tooth.

I take the tunnel that leads to the Sojourner. Since there's nowhere to go and nothing to do here, everyone can usually be found there after dinner. It's not like they have much of a choice. It's the only bar on Mars.

The place is packed, and when I open the door, a blast of warm air hits me.

The bar itself is a long piece of one of the early shuttles that came to Mars. It only made one trip, and then it blew an engine. It was a lousy shuttle, but it's a pretty cool bar.

Sammy the bartender is polishing the surface with a wet cloth when I grab a stool. He nods when he sees me. "Hey, Georgiana. How's it going?"

My real name is Georgiana, but I prefer Georgie. Not that it matters. I've learned that people pretty much call you what they want.

"Okay."

"The usual?"

The usual is a cherry cola, but I have other ideas tonight. After all, in a few short hours I will be fifteen.

"Uh, no," I say, looking around. I put my elbows on the bar and try to look casual, like I've done this before. "I was thinking maybe a beer."

"A beer?" Sammy asks, raising a skeptical eyebrow.

"Yes," I say, struggling to keep my voice from wavering. "A beer."

He shakes his head at me, a stern expression on his face. "You know I can't serve you. You're too young, Georgiana."

"It's not like I'm gonna get drunk and get in a driving accident or anything," I say, exasperated.

The guy next to me, Merrick, says, "You trying to buy a beer, Georgiana?"

"No," I whisper fiercely, looking down.

Merrick's a cellular biologist, and has like ten Ph.D.'s so you'd think he'd be a little perceptive, right? Instead, he turns to the room and announces loudly, "Hey every-one! Our little Georgiana's trying to buy a beer."

The bar bursts into hoots of laughter and clapping and shouts. I put my hands over my face, wishing I could just disappear.

I mean, this is my life.

I can't even sneak my first beer without the entire planet knowing.

The only reason I'm even here is because my father is a geologist, and the last batch of geologists they sent up got killed in a spring dust storm, and since then the geologists aren't exactly lining up to go to Mars anymore. Also because most of the geologists who got killed had once been students of my father. He's one of the only geologists in the world who knows anything about Mars because he was on the original exploratory missions.

After the Spring Disaster, as the media called it, the government begged my father to go back to Mars, which he wanted to do anyway. You could see it in his eyes every time they sent up a new batch of settlers. His one condition was that I come.

You would think I'd be pretty happy to go to Mars. I mean, it's kind of like every kid's dream, right? But I can't stop thinking about water. Anything to do with water. Like going for a swim or taking a shower or even having a real bath.

Because we don't have any water.

Once every two months a shuttle arrives with drinking water, but that's only a supplement. See, our main source of water is from recycling. You got it. We recycle everything—the water you spit out when you brush your teeth, the leftover water from washing dishes, even when you pee—it all gets filtered and put back into the system, and everybody gets a daily ration. It tastes awful, and there's never enough to do anything more than take a sponge bath. Trust me, there's a good reason we're always wearing hats in the television broadcasts.

That's why my father's here in the first place. To find water. The geologists who died in the Spring Disaster were near the south polar cap looking for water when the dust storm hit. It's not as easy as you'd think to find water. Some whiz of a scientist told NASA that they should "Follow the water," that is, follow the scientific evidence of where it's been before, to find new water. Unfortunately they think this planet was once covered with an ocean, so that's a lot of territory to cover. Which is why they need the geologists.

Once they find the water, they can start fixing up the planet, and then lots of people can come. It will be a whole new world for people to mess up and overpopulate.

I mean, I know we're here for a good reason, but speaking from personal experience, who cares about saving mankind when you can't wash your hair?

My parents are waiting for me when I get back to the cabin.

I groan when I see the expression on their faces. News travels fast on a planet where there are only two hundred and three people, and I figure they've heard about my trying to buy a beer.

I start to explain. "Look," I say, "I just wanted a sip. It wasn't anything serious—"

"Georgiana," my mother says in a calm voice. Too calm. "We just got a transmission from Earth."

This isn't what I was expecting.

"We weren't even going to tell you, but—"

"But what?" I'm getting a bad feeling here.

My father takes off his glasses and cleans them with a corner of his shirt. He puts them back on and says wearily, "Nana's been diagnosed with stomach cancer."

"She's dying," my mother says.

Nana was the one who taught me how to swim.

All those summers my parents spent at NASA, or on the International Space Station, I'd go to the Jersey Shore and live with Nana in her sweet little yellow house looking out on the beach. Truth be told, those summers were the best parts of my life. I looked forward to them all year. Part of me still wishes I could have just lived with Nana forever.

"Your parents love you," she always says, and I know they do, but it's like they weren't the right kind of people to have kids. You can just see that they forget I'm here sometimes, like an experiment that's slipped their minds. Especially my dad. We look nothing alike, and I swear there are days when even I wonder if I'm someone else's baby they picked up in the hospital by mistake. I mean, I'm almost fifteen and he still hasn't figured out that I hate to be called Georgiana.

But Nana knows everything about me. My dreams, my goals, my fears. Stuff that I could never tell my parents. Like how I wanted to get a place on the swim team (I did), and that I was worried my folks would pressure me to become a scientist like them (they did), and how I wished a cute boy named Chen would kiss me (he did, behind the gym at school—it was very nice).

The truth is, she's the thing I miss the most from Earth. Sure, I hate the dust, and not being able to take a bath or have a conversation with someone my own age, but there are days when I think I'll go crazy from the loneliness of not being able to talk to her. And every time I dream about water, I dream of Nana and me together.

The two mermaids in the middle of the ocean.

I just know she'd laugh at the way we live in plastic tents. "Why, you all look like hamsters," she'd say, and she'd be right. She's just that kind of person. She tells it like it is.

She's the only person in the whole world who's ever believed in me.

And they weren't going to tell me?

"So when are we going back?" I say.

"We're not," my mom says.

"What are you talking about? We can't just leave Nana alone." Nana is my father's mother, and he's an only child. We're all she has.

"Honey," my mom says. "We talked to the doctors. The cancer's already spread to her lymph nodes. She's only got five months to live. We'd never make it back in time. She'll die before we get there."

"You don't know that for sure! You're just guessing," I say.

My dad, ever the compassionate scientist, says, "Statistically speaking, there's only a five percent chance that Nana would survive more than five months, especially given her complications."

I mean, this is how they talk.

"Well I don't care. I'm going."

"You can't go," my mom says. "Your last calcium test came back and"—and here she takes a deep breath—"and it seems that you've lost over thirty percent of your bone density."

"So what? I'll drink a lot of milk, okay?" Actually, I hate milk, especially the powdered kind we have on Mars, but I'll do anything to get back to Nana.

"You don't understand, Georgiana," my father says. "You've lost thirty percent of your bone mass. No one knows what effect that will have when you get back to Earth. Your legs could shatter from the gravity, and you may never walk again."

"You could be in a wheelchair for the rest of your life," my mother adds helpfully.

"But," I say, my voice wavering, "didn't you know about this before you brought me up here?"

My parents cast a sidelong glance at each other, and it's clear that neither one of these brilliant scientists thought this one through.

"So how am I ever gonna leave Mars?" I whisper.

My dad, Mr. Mars himself, just looks at me and says quizzically, "Why would you want to leave?"

Like Nana always said, just because you have brains, it doesn't mean you have sense.

I'm sitting at a table in the mess hall eating breakfast and generally trying to avoid everyone. It's gotten around that I tried to buy a beer last night, and I'm getting a lot of condescending warnings about the perils of alcohol. I want to say that I think a sip of beer is hardly the most life-threatening thing considering I just found out all my bones are going to melt if I ever go back to earth.

"Hey, brat."

I look up and see Buddy standing there holding a tray.

Buddy is twenty-one, and a marine. Everyone here is either a scientist or in the military. Some paranoid politician back in Washington seems to think that another country might get it into their heads to send a shuttle up here to claim a chunk of Mars to use as a military outpost. In my opinion, anyone who actually *wants* to come to a planet where you can't take a bath is too stupid to be much of a national security threat.

Buddy's hair is cut short in a buzz, and the skin on his face is dry and flaky, which isn't any surprise because mine is the same way. When there's no water on a planet, it's hard to keep your skin moist and glowing. Still, I like Buddy. He's funny, and even though he's a marine, he's one of the few adults who doesn't talk to me like I'm a little kid or an idiot.

He sits down, starts digging into his rehydrated eggs. "Dust storm's coming," he says.

What else is new.

I pick up a toffee candy that they leave out in bowls on all the tables at every meal. People eat them like crazy. I mean, if there was no toffee, there'd be like a rebellion or a mutiny or something.

"How's it going?" he asks, pausing to look up.

"I've had better days," I say.

Buddy squints across at me. "Heard about last night."

I don't say anything.

"I wouldn't worry about it. People like to talk," he says in a consoling voice. "By the way, happy birthday."

"I don't care about last night," I say.

"Oh?"

"My grandmother has cancer. She's gonna die. In five months."

He blinks. "Whoa. That's terrible."

I shake my head. "She's always been so healthy. She was an Olympic swimmer."

"No kidding."

I nod. "She won a gold medal. Backstroke." And then it all comes out in a painful rush. "My parents refuse to go back to Earth to see her. They say she's going to die before they get there, and they won't let me go because apparently I've lost thirty percent of my bones and they think my body will shatter or something."

He puts down his fork, sits back. "Talk about a lousy birthday present."

"No kidding."

"Why did they even bring you?"

Good question.

"Maybe you should leave now, you know, before it gets any worse. Have you talked to the doc about it yet?"

"No," I say. "It doesn't matter, though. My parents won't let me go."

"You can always stow away," he says jokingly. "That's what my grandfather did."

"What do you mean?"

"My grandfather grew up on a farm, and he hated it, so he ran away and stowed aboard a navy ship. Ended up in Hawaii." His beeper goes off, and he looks down. "Gotta go, brat. Ask the doc."

I stare at him. I don't exactly have a lot of faith in adults these days. Especially the ones who suck my blood out.

"Ask the doc," Buddy says again. He stands up, pockets a handful of toffees and winks at me. "I just love this candy. Takes the taste of dust away."

He buckles into his suit and disappears out the door.

Even though I live on a planet with some of the smartest scientists in the world, I swear it's the most intelligent conversation I've had in months.

"Nobody really knows what will happen to you. You're the first adolescent to live on Mars, Georgiana," the doctor says, as he looks at me from behind his big desk.

Like I don't know this already? Trust me, I am very

well aware that there's not a boy within sixty-seven million miles who can kiss me.

"What's the worst-case scenario?" I ask.

His gaze doesn't waver. "Your leg bones will shatter from
the force of Earth's gravity and you'll never walk again."

I let that sink in. "Okay, what else could happen?"

He leans back in his chair, folds his hands. "Your legs
would sustain massive fractures and you'd spend months in a
full body cast. In the best-case scenario, you wouldn't sustain
any breaks and would only require hospitalization to build
up your calcium."

"How long would that be?"

He purses his lips, considering. "A minimum of four to
five months, I imagine, on a full regimen of IV-delivered
drugs. It will take at least that long to build up some of the
lost calcium. And even after that you'll have to be very careful and restrict your activity. Physical therapy, too, I imagine."
He shrugs. "It's really hard to say."

Is he serious? Four to five months in a hospital with a needle
in my arm? I hate needles, I really do, especially after spending
the last year being poked and prodded and measured.

"What would you do if you were me?" I ask the doctor.

"Ah," he says. "But I'm not you."

And that's when I realize I'm in this alone.

"Sweetie," my mom says a few days later as I lay in my bunk.
"We know you're feeling a bit down about Nana, so your dad has
a little birthday surprise for you. Don't you, honey?"

"Well," he says excitedly. "I got permission for us to take a rover out!"

I roll my eyes. Just what I need. Another rock-hunting expedition.

"I'm really not up to looking at rocks," I say.

"But we're not going to look at rocks," he says. "It's even better."

This should be good. My dad's idea of a fun time is taking core samples.

"Come on," my mother says, tugging me up. "I promise you'll like it."

My dad drives the rover out. We are wearing our survival suits, breathing an air mixture.

He parks the rover, gets out, and starts walking away from us, but I just stare. We are all alone in the middle of Mars and it's strange how serene it is—the horizon unbroken by buildings or trees or anything but a rolling rock-studded surface, an alien desert.

"This way," my dad calls over his mike. "Race you to the edge!"

And then we are bounding across the landscape and I'm leaping over big boulders with an ease I could never have done on Earth and it's such a rush, this feeling coursing through me, my heart pounding, my lungs inflating, as if every cell in me is shouting—so healthy! so alive!—that it seems inconceivable that this same strong body may not support me on Earth.

I stop suddenly, my dad a step ahead, my breath caught in

my throat. We are standing on the edge of a huge canyon, winding and wild, something out of a movie. It is the most beautiful thing I have ever seen, I think. It's awesome in its rawness, like the ocean, and a strange peace steals over me.

"That," my dad says, "is the Nirgal Vallis. We think there was once a big river there."

"Like the Grand Canyon?" I say.

"Exactly, Georgiana," my mom says.

"And see right there? That red flag?" my dad says, pointing to a stretch of cliff where a little red flag waves merrily.

"Uh-huh."

He clears his throat importantly. "That little spot is where I found a downward smear of water-soluble mineral deposits in a core sample." He draws the moment out. "I figure we drill about four hundred meters down and we'll hit water," he says with a wink.

"Really?" Even I can't keep the excitement out of my voice. *They found water!*

"Really," my mom says, smiling at my dad proudly. "Your dad's a smart guy." She grasps his hand.

"Does anybody know yet?" I ask.

"Not yet. We won't announce it until we know for sure," my dad says.

"But we will," my mom adds confidently.

"The signs are all there," he says.

I stare at my dad. "But how do you know you'll find water, Dad? I mean, how can you know for sure?"

And then he says something that shocks me.

"Nothing's ever certain, Georgiana," my dad, the scientist, says. His voice crackles over the mike. "You just have to have hope."

I'm bobbing in the ocean, my wet hair plastering my face, the scent of salt in the air. The water's warm, and I turn and there is Nana right beside me.

"Nana," I cry, hugging her tight, embracing her sturdy body, comforting like Christmas. "I've missed you so."

"Why, I've missed you, too, Georgie," she says, pushing a strand of hair out of my face.

"You don't look like you're dying," I say.

"Who said I was dying? I'm healthy as a horse!"

And she looks it. Her cheeks are ruddy, her skin is flush with good health, even her eyes are shining.

"I want to do something," I say. "But I'm a little scared."

"You can do whatever you want to do," she says. "You always could."

"I want to come home," I say simply. "And be with you."

"But, Georgie," she says, her eyes twinkling, "you're already home."

And then I wake up alone in the dark little plastic cabin and hear the dust storm raging outside and I can't help myself.

I just cry.

Buddy sidles up to me in the mess hall with a full tray of food. People are lingering over their precious cups of coffee and chewing on toffees.

"You been crying, brat?"

I glare at him.

"So did you see the doc?" he presses.

"Yeah. Great news. Best-case scenario I have to be in a hospital for four or five months hooked up to an IV. Worst case, I'm crippled for life." I swallow hard. "And Nana's all alone," I whisper, my voice breaking.

He clears his throat. "My grandfather died from cancer too. They gave him three months to live. And you know how long he lasted?"

"How long?" I whisper, hope lodged in my throat.

"A whole year."

I'd settle for a week with Nana, I think.

His beeper goes off and he groans. "There goes dinner. Shuttle just got in."

"Shuttle?"

"Supply shuttle. I'm helping to unload it. It's on a quick turnaround. Just dropping off supplies and then heading back to Earth in the morning." He stands abruptly.

The dust storm is roaring outside, but the only thing I hear is that one little word.

Earth.

I grab his wrist. "Maybe I could bring you some coffee in the morning. You know, over at the shuttle," I say casually, looking him straight in the eye, willing him to hear me.

Buddy unwraps a toffee, sticks it in his mouth, chews for a moment, and stares at me. There's a curious expression on his face.

"Sure," he says finally. "How about at oh-seven-hundred?"

Over his shoulder, I see my parents enter the cafeteria, holding hands and laughing, and something inside me goes still. Suddenly, all these little things seem so important—this candy, those smiles, these two strong legs. How can I possibly give this up?

Buddy sees where I'm looking and shakes his head.

"You sure you know what you're doing? Have you thought about it? You know, your legs?" he asks.

"Nothing's certain," I say, and know that I am my father's daughter after all. "But you just have to have hope."

The next morning when I wake up my parents are getting ready to head out.

"Your dad and I are going out with the Alpha team to Nirgal Vallis. We won't be back until late tonight," my mom says excitedly.

She is wearing her exploration suit, and she looks so happy, like she's about to burst.

"This is it, Georgie," she whispers, her face one big grin. "I know we're going to find water today. You'll have your very own pool in no time at all!"

"I know you will too," I say, and can't help but think how ironic it is that I'm leaving this planet just when it's getting good.

Still, I hug her hard. "I love you, Mom."

My dad's almost out the door when I stop him, hug him hard too. He's startled.

"Good luck," I say.

And then they are gone.

Buddy is waiting for me when I bring over the thermos of coffee. It's the beginning of the shift and he's the only one there.

"Hey, brat," he says.

"Hey, Buddy," I blush, holding my duffel.

"The closet in the back is cleared out for you. Door's open. There's a blanket and some other stuff there too."

"Here," I say, and give him my dog-eared copy of *Red Mars* by Kim Stanley Robinson.

He raises a curious eyebrow.

"It's this science fiction book," I say, "about the first colonists on Mars."

Buddy laughs at me. "Does he get it right?"

I grin back. "Sort of. Although I kind of like his version better."

Buddy nods.

I hesitate for a moment, stare down at my legs. Can I really do this? I mean, talk about deserving a sip of beer.

He pats my cheek, and says, "Don't worry. You'll be fine. Just have them hook you up in the same hospital your grandmother's in. That way you can be together. It won't be so bad."

"Thanks," I whisper.

"You better get moving, brat. The captain's just about finishing breakfast now." He gives me a goofy little grin. "And hey, take a swim for me, okay?"

"Only if you take one for me," I say, and he shoots me a quizzical look.

"What?" he asks, but I just smile mysteriously at him. He'll know what I mean soon enough.

After all, news travels fast on this planet.

As the engines roar to life I settle back and close my eyes, imagining Mars disappearing behind me, and all that blue water ahead. A whole world of it. And there, in the middle of it all, is Nana with her warm smile and steady eyes.

I can almost hear her voice. "Georgie," she will say. "It's heaven to be here with you."

They should be finding my note right about now, I figure.

TESTING, TESTING, 1 . . . 2 . . . 3

A. LaFaye

LAST SPRING I HAD ONE CHANCE OF GETTING INTO HIGH SCHOOL THE FOLLOWING YEAR—PASSING THE EIGHTH GRADE STANDARDIZED TESTS. I DID SO BADLY on the pretests they started to call me the Idiot of Seville. That's where I'm from, a town called Seville.

But I'm not an idiot. I'm really not. Long ago the Greeks used to say an idiot was a guy who didn't know anything about other cultures. I know a lot about other cultures. Heck, I just explained what the ancient Greeks meant when they called some guy an idiot.

When the kids at school called me an idiot, they meant the kind of stupid jerk who couldn't even pass stinking old pretests. I did so bad on those things Mr. Henshaw, the guidance counselor, sent me in to be tested for a learning disability—again.

I'm not so good at reading textbooks, doing homework, or taking tests. Don't get me wrong, I love to learn new stuff. It's just that the stuff I want to learn doesn't show up in textbooks or on tests. Actually, I used to do great on tests. I'd whiz through them and be done in enough time to get back to the book I was reading.

Nowadays I get kind of lost inside the test. I read a question like what was the importance of the Continental Congress? Then I get to thinking about the delegates who stood in that congress demanding a stop to taxation without representation while they held slaves. Who represented their slaves? Why couldn't they see that those African people had undeniable rights too? What about women? And the poor? Did they really just want the power for themselves? To keep the money they paid in taxes?

See what I mean? I get lost when I'm taking a test. I never finish them anymore. In those pretests, I got most of the questions I answered right, but I only answered about a quarter of them.

Mr. Henshaw figured I had a learning disability that made it hard for me to read and take tests. But the people who tested me for that just said I didn't apply myself. That diagnosis sent my dad through the roof.

In fact, he cornered me on the roof just outside my room. I was out there working on a star map when he crawled out and planted himself next to me. He sat there for a minute staring, then said, "School's like learning to play an instrument,

Patrick. You never get good at it if you don't practice to the point of hating it. You've really got to commit to it. Or you could end up the only thirty-year-old eighth grader."

"You spend a lot of time on that speech?" I asked.

He laughed. "Practice makes perfect."

And he wanted me to "practice" my homework every night, all night. He even threatened to take away my mowing job until my grades got better. That would've been a real killer. I did my best thinking while mowing. The engine noise cut out the rest of the world and I just let her rip—mentally speaking. I mowed on autopilot. Thought about all the things I'd been studying—taxation without representation, brown dwarf stars, and Pythagoras's theorem. I'd been mowing the same lawns for four years, so I could mow them by memory.

Except for Mrs. Whittamore's lawn. I had just started mowing for her a week after the pretests. She hired me through the mail. That may seem odd, but I get a lot of weird stuff in the mail. When I hit second grade, I started getting a blank card each week. I didn't know who sent them. There was never a return address on the envelope. No postmark. Just my name. Each one was a different blind-you bright color, but they never had one word on the card inside. Mrs. Whittamore's card was bright too. There was no return address. I even thought it was another blank card, but instead she asked me to mow her lawn for her every Saturday at noon.

Hiring someone through the mail's a little weird, but not for Mrs. Whittamore. Everyone said she was a witch. When I went to elementary school, my friends and I had to walk by her place every day. Kids told all sorts of creepy tales about her, hung witch's claw roots along her front fence. Those little creeps even threw rotten eggs at her house on Halloween. I never did any of that crazy stuff. I just wanted to know what her yard really looked like. Except for the narrow strip in front of her house, her whole yard was hidden from view by nine-foot hedges.

No one I knew ever saw behind those hedges. In fact, no one ever saw Mrs. Whittamore, not even her neighbor Mrs. Clausen. I mow her lawn too. She's always telling me stories about her eerie neighbor. Like how she sees an odd blue glow in Mrs. Whittamore's cupola at night and the strange chiming that echoes from the old woman's house on occasion.

Mrs. Whittamore stays well hidden behind those hedges. And the chance to get a look on the other side of them was exactly what made me accept the job even though she wrote that she planned to pay me with only a book.

At five to noon that Saturday, I pushed my mower up to her front porch, then went up to ring the bell and see where she wanted me to start. Only the screen door stood between me and her front hall, which led straight down the center of the house to a back door. I could see the green leaves of her hedges through the screen door in the back.

The whole house looked shadowy and dark. No one answered the bell. A gust of wind came up, rustled the ivy along the front wall and blew the screen door wide open. I expected it to bang shut, but it hung open. I stepped into the hallway to give Mrs. Whittamore a shout, figuring she might be hard of hearing. The front door clanked shut as I called for her.

The wind swooshed through each room as I walked down the hall, calling out. You'd think that breeze meant to hurry me through the house the way it swept along behind me. It even opened the back door.

I stepped out onto the porch and froze. The entire back-yard was a carpet of flower rings. Rust-colored mums grew in the center, ringed by blue fuzzy flowers surrounded by pink daises. The different kinds of flowers rippled right up to the edge of the porch. I'd never seen such a thing in my life. No wonder she kept her yard hedged in. If she didn't, the place would be crowded with gawkers.

The sound of someone clearing her throat turned me around. Mrs. Whittamore sat in a wicker chair, her long legs flung over an arm with a book plopped in her lap. I expected a proper old lady with her gray hair in a bun, who wore fancy old-fashioned flowery dresses and brooches. Instead she wore short pants covered in stars and no shoes. Her gray hair hung over her shoulders.

"Hello, I'm Patrick Troy. I've come to do your lawn. Do you want me to start in front?"

She pointed to an old-fashioned push mower with the whirly blades, sitting next to a porcupine statue standing at the edge of her backyard. Old people like to use old things. No problem. That gave me more time to think over my study guide for the big tests.

"You want me to use that out front?"

She shook her head, then pointed to the flower circles.

Why didn't she talk to me? Was she mute? Did she really want me to cut down all those great-looking flowers? "You want me to mow your flowers?"

Nodding, she held up a card. It looked blank. I walked closer, figuring she couldn't speak, so I had to read her instructions. As I got up farther, the card seemed to have gray squiggly lines that moved around like curly hair caught in the wind. Standing right in front of her, squinting, the lines darkened and stiffened into letters. I thought I needed to get my eyes checked for new glasses. That happened every spring.

The card read, "The butterflies need exercise." She smiled, her misty eyes getting all shiny.

The old lady had to be nuts. But I didn't want to upset her, so I started mowing her flowers. I felt guilty for cutting them down, then I noticed the butterflies taking flight. In colors as brilliant and varied as the flowers, they took off in all directions like the flower petals had turned into wings. I had to stop and watch them fly. As they flew higher, they looked like bits of confetti headed for the clouds.

Mrs. Whittamore cleared her throat again. When I looked her way, she waved her hand to tell me to get busy.

"Sorry," I said, mowing ahead. The entire sky filled with bright wings as I moved in a circle. I don't know why I did it that way, but it almost felt like I traveled down a spiral slide that kept pushing me forward. By the time I had the back lawn done, I felt dizzy. I had to lie down for a minute, but it gave me chance to see the last of the butterflies fly off.

The backyard looked like the school gym after a dance. Instead of shredded streamers, the place was covered in shed petals. As I stepped onto the porch, Mrs. Whittamore stood up to hand me the book she'd been reading. I felt like a dwarf. She towered over me and I'm already five foot ten. I'd never seen such a giant woman before—no wonder why she needed such a tall hedge to keep her privacy. I took the book.

She held up another card. Even that close up, it looked like the letters swirled. I figured I was still a little dizzy. The card read, "To help you study."

"Thanks," I said, but I was wondering how a hermity old lady knew about the tests. "Same time next Saturday?"

She nodded.

I came out her front door feeling like I'd just walked out of an intense movie and I hadn't quite readjusted to the real world again. I checked my watch to be sure I'd get to Mrs. Clausen's on time. My watch said noon. How could it only be twelve o'clock? There was no way I could've mowed that yard in five minutes. I figured my watch battery had run down again. That happened to me a lot. My mom said it was my magnetic personality. Ha-ha.

I opened the book to see what one she'd given me and discovered that the thing was as blank as the cards I got in the mail. She must've wanted me to use it to take notes while I studied. Pocketing the book, I headed over to Mrs. Clausen's.

After an afternoon of mowing, I went home to study. I studied all week. My dad sent me straight to my room after supper. I had to study there until it was time for bed.

The following Saturday I showed up at Mrs. Whittamore's house ready to mow her front lawn. No one answered the bell. The wind opened the door and whooshed me through the house again. And as before, I stood on the back porch frozen in amazement. The flowers stood as tall and bright as if they'd been growing all spring. I turned to Mrs. Whittamore, hoping she could tell me how she made flowers grow like mutant weeds. She stood next to me, holding a card. In my shock, the letters looked all swimmy. Getting ahold of myself, I could read, "Did you enjoy the book?"

"Oh yeah, it's great for taking notes."

"Taking notes?!" The words nearly sprang off the card. How did she write so fast? I didn't even see her take out a pen.

"The book was blank. I thought it was for note taking."

"That book is as blank as this card."

Right then I realized my eyes had seen everything clearly, only my mind had been out of focus. The words on that card did change and move. Mrs. Whittamore never stopped to write. Her thoughts just leapt onto the card. She really was a witch and she'd given *me* a magic book. I wanted to run home and read it, but Mrs. Whittamore's card read, "Do your work, then study."

I nodded, saying, "Thank you, thank you."

Spinning through the flowers I sent the butterflies to wing

and gave them their aerobatic exercise. Then I rushed off to finish the other lawns, my mind constantly wondering what kinds of secrets that book really held.

Finally I made it home and to my room so I could crack that book open. I saw no words. Not even a smudge. I squinted, tilted the book, looked at it through a magnifying glass—nothing worked. I'm no warlock, I told myself. The only one who could read that book was Mrs. Whittamore. Why'd she even give it to me? I threw the book into a corner and ignored it all week.

I went back to Mrs. Whittamore's the next Saturday, but the front door was shut. The note on it said, "Come back only after you've read from the book. I don't want my butterflies cared for by any simpleminded dolt. Stop relying on your eyes. Use your head. The magic's in the moment itself."

Mowing Mrs. Clausen's yard that afternoon, I tried to figure out what Mrs. Whittamore was trying to tell me. The magic's in the moment itself. What's that supposed to mean? Sure, I'd gotten lost in the moment before—drifted from the Continental Congress to a plantation in the Carolinas but where's the magic in that?

Staring into the grass in front of me, I let myself drift into the greenness of it, hoping that getting lost in that one moment would show me something. I tried again. The whips of the blades slowed like those on a helicopter just after the engine's been turned off. And there, in midwing flap, hung a blue butterfly. I'd captured it in a moment.

I didn't even finish Mrs. Clausen's yard. I ran straight home. Flopping down on my bed with the book, I stared at the page and let my mind drift into it. Words rose up like growing plants. It read, "Magic in the Middle Ages was as commonplace as prayer."

I pulled the words up and they kept right on going. I read about kitchen spells to make the bread rise, the sour milk go good, the random cut heal without infection. I read until my mind filled up like a computer disk. I could've sworn I heard a ding like a warning message—this brain is full.

I'd read half the book. Usually it'd take me all day to read that much. But when I looked at the clock, hardly any time had passed. I'd stayed in the moment through half the book. I wanted to announce my talent. Tell everyone I knew. Who would believe me? Mrs. Whittamore, that's who.

I ran over there. Her doors stood open. I found her waiting for me on the back porch. Babbling, I started to tell her everything. She smiled, her eyebrows arched, and held up a note: "Congratulations, now get to work."

I could've flown behind that mower. In fact, I'm not so sure I didn't.

As I left, Mrs. Whittamore passed me a note: "Don't neglect your duties, Patty. Magic thins when you're not responsible."

"Okay. I won't," I shouted on my way to finish Mrs. Clausen's lawn.

That night, as I read on about magic, Dad came in with a plate of sandwiches to check on me. "You studying, Patrick?"

I raised the book to say, "Yeah, sure, Dad." But Mrs. Whittamore's words echoed back to me. "Don't neglect your duties, Patty."

I was sure no questions about magic would show up on the tests, so I said, "I'll get right to it, Dad."

Biting into a sandwich, Dad said, "Good to hear it."

Putting the book aside, I gathered up all of my textbooks and my study guide, then set to work. Trying to get lost into the school books just made my head ache. A strange thumping caught my attention. The cover of Mrs. Whittamore's book flapped like a wing. Opening it up, I found a note card sticking out of the crease. It read, "Why walk when you can fly?" in Mrs. Whittamore's flowing hand.

Staring into the book, I dove into the American Revolution. Everything appeared in that book—maps of battles, conditions of hospitals, forts, and prisons. I read about officers, infantry men, women on the homefront, women who marched into battle as men, slaves who fought for their right to be free, children who studied the war firsthand. I knew salaries, strategies, and sailing techniques for delivering supplies.

As soon as a question rose in my mind, an answer sprawled out on the page. I journeyed through the entire war in one night. I traveled into the realm of mathematics next, then science after that. I not only learned equations, theories, and discoveries, but the histories behind them—the origins of numbers, the lives of the people who mapped out the mysteries of the world.

And at school, when a teacher handed out a unit test, I dove into the moment, wading my way through each question at my own speed. When I came up with my own question, I scribbled it on a piece of scratch paper to look it up later. I finished each test in ten minutes or less, then kept writing on my scratch paper so the teacher wouldn't suspect anything.

On Saturdays, Mrs. Whittamore and I talked as I mowed. Her words appeared on a pad of paper hanging off the mower handle. She told me how she noticed me as a child. I was the only one who didn't gawk or leave roots or throw rotten eggs. She'd often seen me passing with my nose in a book, heard the questions as they formed in my head. She'd been sending me letters for years, waiting for me to be ready to read them.

So that's who sent me those blank cards. They weren't blank after all. I thanked Mrs. Whittamore, but she said having company who could understand her was all the thanks she needed.

Boy, can I see how important it is to have someone who understands you. Thanks to Mrs. Whittamore's understanding of how I learned, I took my own time in finishing those standardized tests. Not only did I pass them, but I ranked so high up in the state that they finally realized how much school bored me and let me skip a grade. Now I'm the only fourteen-year-old sophomore at Seville High. I'm willing to bet I'm the only kid in all of Seville who knows how to make butterflies glad to fly.

TEA PARTY ENDS IN
BLOODY MASSACRE, FILM AT 11

———————

Gregory Maguire

"IT'S A SHAME," SAID THE TUFTED PLUM IN A WHISPER.

"It's more than a shame. It's a disgrace," replied the Anemic Giraffe.

"Everywhere you look, nothing but *books*. Not a shred of tatting, appliquéing, embroidery, stenciling, patchwork. No crossstitching of improving statements, no arrangement of dried flowers."

Her mother's visitors didn't know that Henrietta was hiding under the dining-room table. Up above on the new lace cloth squatted a lopsided berry tart topped with a crown of meringue. A dozen flowery cups were centered in a dozen matching flowery saucers. Lemon slices lay pinwheeled on a pink plate. Down below in the gloom sprawled Henrietta

Mott with a copy of *Chiller Thriller 14: The Thing That Lasts.*

"Does it show a lack of concern for the telling household detail? I thought I saw *Soviet Decay: The Commerce of Anarchy.* Very heady stuff."

"Perhaps it belongs to her husband."

"Don't you mean *belonged?*"

"I believe you understood my meaning. I notice no recent issues of *Higher Values Through Better Housekeeping.*"

"Maybe the subscription hasn't been forwarded yet."

"Do you think she's one to get out and plant daffodils along the tennis courts?"

"We'll just have to see. Looks like a good tart, anyway."

The Anemic Giraffe sniffed. "Architecturally speaking, it lists."

"*Shh.* Here she comes."

Mrs. Mott came into the room. At least, the best shoes of Mrs. Mott came into the room, and ankles and calves that looked like Mrs. Mott's came too. That was all Henrietta could see. But she knew, because she had watched her mother getting ready, that the outfit was new and pretty and not much like Mrs. Mott. It swished and swirled, and Mrs. Mott's usual overalls rarely swished and swirled, except in the washing machine.

"I'm sorry," said the voice of Mrs. Mott. "I'd wanted you to meet my daughter Henrietta. She was looking forward to saying hello. Maybe she went out to the treehouse. I'll just go grab the teapot and give a holler out back. Do make yourselves comfortable."

Away went the good shoes and stockinged legs of Mrs. Mott.

"Can't keep track of her own daughter? Is that wise?" Tufted Plum sniffed.

"Out back? In a treehouse? Isn't that against community code?"

"Not a tomboy, I hope. Daughter *or* mother. And I must say I've never 'given a holler out back' in all my born days."

"One wouldn't know how."

Very quietly Henrietta turned the page to chapter seven. Her tiny penlight made a circle of light on the text.

Slowly the Thing That Lasts lifted what was left of its chins. Its body was of its own making, repaired with whatever came to hand. Its skeletal limbs were loosely sheathed in the pelts of meadow creatures and pets whose bad luck it had been to cross its path. Its head was tethered onto its spine by cords of animal muscle twisted together and strengthened by power lines torn off poles. It was hungry. It wanted blood. The Thing That Lasts always wanted blood. It sniffed hungrily through nostrils that gaped and flared.

Mrs. Mott returned. "Oh, you'd have liked Henrietta. She's an original. I only hope she'll return before it's time for you to go. Now, please, let me pour you some tea. Milk? Sugar? Lemon?"

"Lemon and sugar both, two lumps."

"I'll have the same. You're too kind."

Henrietta could hear the new silver tongs rattle against the pink plate. Her mother must be nervous. Her hand was shaking. Why? Surely the two Local League ladies couldn't be anywhere near as frightening as the Thing That Lasts?

"Perhaps we'll just sit here in the window nook," said Mrs. Mott. "It's so much cozier than the parlor."

It's not a *parlor*, it's a *living room*, thought Henrietta. But she knew why her mother would want to avoid it. The living room had been arranged with a dozen chairs, some borrowed from the new church. Why were there only two Local League ladies here?

"It's so nice to welcome a new neighbor." Tufted Plum sounded admiring of herself.

"One finds this is a very discriminating community." Anemic Giraffe sniffed the tea delicately but dubiously, as if the bouquet didn't meet her expectations.

"I see," said Mrs. Mott.

Henrietta had always been taught that discrimination was wrong, but maybe there was more than one kind. If she leaned to one side and peered around the leg of the dining-room table, she could see the Local League ladies. Tufted Plum was stout and severe, lost in a rucking of purple and rose ruffles. Tiny pearl earrings that looked like beads of milk clung to her earlobes. Anemic Giraffe was slim and severe, clad closely in acid yellow. Her shiny pointy shoes looked like implements for the torture of stray cats.

I'd like to see what would happen if the Thing That Lasts met up with those two, thought Henrietta. She began to imagine it.

The Thing That Lasts straightened its several spines with a sound of creaking, as a ship's timbers groan and scrape under force of wind and wave. It had four unmatched eyes, two in its head for observing forward locomotion and two in its ears, so it could see what it was hearing. All the eyes blinked dryly. Outside the strictly clean new house in the strictly fancy new neighborhood it lumbered, slobbering in the strictly tended yew bushes. It could see two Local League ladies perched on chairs, in full and tantalizing view in a bay window. Like lobsters in a tank. The Thing That Lasts puckered its scabby lips. A flayed bit of tongue unraveled. Distracted, the Thing That Lasts bit off part of its tongue and spit it on the ground, and began to lurch and slope across the strictly manicured lawn.

"I suppose you'll be wondering about our organization."
"It's so kind of you to call," said Mrs. Mott.
"The Local League ladies always call on new families."
"It's the thing Local League ladies do."
"One of the things."
"Local Leagues are very prestigious organizations."
"Have you ever belonged to a Local League before?"
Mrs. Mott stirred her tea. She paused as if thinking over a long and busy social life, which in fact she had always enjoyed. But she had never encountered Local League ladies on the Upper West Side of Manhattan, and Henrietta knew it. "No," said Mrs. Mott conclusively, "I have never belonged to

a Local League. Can you explain to me what it is?"

"A Local League is an informal club of right-minded women who do good and uphold standards."

"A Local League is a chapter of feminine powerhouses wreaking taste and order wherever it finds itself." This must be something of a joke, as Anemic Giraffe snorted an inelegant giggle at her own wit.

"I see," said Mrs. Mott, who had worked very hard to make sure that her berry tart was both tasteful and orderly, but failed.

"You see, a great deal of nonsense is advanced these days about equality between the sexes. Local League ladies think this is balderdash."

"Poppycock."

"Stuff and nonsense."

"And then some."

"Men and women equal? Absurd."

"Women are far superior. As we all know. But our chiefest strength lies in disguising that fact and working behind the lines of power."

"Like spies in the ointment."

"Like *agents provocateurs* in the mob."

"We rabble-rouse when we must, but always in dulcet tones."

"We believe that boys will be boys and girls should be girls, that men are men and women are smarter."

"And all this fuss about girls on sports teams and boys doing ballet! Men raising babies and women fighting fires! Men baking rosemary focaccia from scratch and women chairing important Senate subcommittees! It's very popular but it's a trend that won't last."

"We're preserving the time-honored notions so there's something to return to when, at last, the world comes to its senses."

"This is lovely tea."

They smacked their lips in the most ladylike way. Mrs. Mott, who liked nothing better than tarring the roof to keep the rain out, smiled palely.

"Your daughter, we trust, is the soul of decorum."

"The very picture of docile sweetness."

"We've so been looking forward to meeting her."

"And she you," said Mrs. Mott in a faint voice, though this was not true at all.

The Thing That Lasts hobbled on buckling haunches and leered in the window. It saw a couple of convenient dabs of lunch cawing away with cups of tea in their hands. One was stout and severe. The other was slim and severe. They'd serve as savory hors d'oeuvres. The Thing That Lasts was feeling peckish.

"Tell us about your little Henrietta."

"The darling."

Mrs. Mott sighed. Henrietta knew she was thinking about Henrietta's Greatest Moments in the old neighborhood. Henrietta's annual Mud Wrestling Competition. Henrietta's Circus of Freaks and Dreads. Henrietta's handwritten monthly neighborhood newspaper, *The Timely Tattler.* The various times cops had come to the house, more bemused than agitated. The principal's visit. The several broken limbs (all by accident, not design). Henrietta's debut camcorder masterpiece: *Himalayan Hijack: Film at 11.*

"She's a little sugarpie," said Mrs. Mott. Henrietta buckled in disbelief and nearly knocked her head against the table, giving herself away. A little sugarpie is the *last* thing she would have called herself.

"How lovely for you."

"What a comfort in your time of distress."

Mrs. Mott didn't like to talk about her time of distress. She said, "Let me go look out the back door again. Surely she's lollygagging nearby. She knew you were coming to call." She backed out the door and disappeared into the kitchen.

"Poor thing," said Tufted Plum.

"A well-trained daughter can be a solace." Anemic Giraffe delivered herself of this bromide with a tidy smirk.

Henrietta knew what they were talking about. Though Mrs. Mott tried to keep a low profile, the story of Mr. Mott was too well known. He was detained in a rugged landlocked foreign country in Central Asia, a new cowboy republic of oppressed peasants governed by former Soviet mafiosi. Mr. Mott had been accused falsely of espionage. He'd been in a prison for more than a year and Mrs. Mott had spent half that year in the distant capital begging for his release. Finally she'd come home, know-ing Henrietta needed her too. And they'd moved to a new neighborhood, a tony, gated community beyond the Beltway in

Virginia, to get away from the cameras, the reporters, the prying neighbors, the possibility of a security breach against their persons by agents of the foreign government.

Mrs. Mott was very alone. The Local League ladies were not really her idea of good company, but even Henrietta knew that Henrietta could be a bit much sometimes. Mrs. Mott needed someone nearby but not too close, until the ambassadors and agents and diplomats managed to spring Mr. Mott out of jail and back into his family's waiting arms.

The Local League ladies seemed rather lo-cal as far as social nutrition went, but if they were all that was on offer and if her mother thought they would do, then Henrietta was prepared to tolerate them. Though they looked like dry sawdust to her. When they began to whisper together, their voices sounded like sawdust rubbing against itself.

"Though I'm known as the spirit of tolerance, Mrs. Mott does seem a bit jittery," proffered Tufted Plum.

"It all hinges on the daughter. If she's one of those tomboy creatures, one would have to vote no," argued Anemic Giraffe.

The Thing That Lasts opened its maw. No constituent parts of it understood about glass, but that didn't matter. It would scissor the broken spears of glass out of its way in one bloody instant as it tore the heart out of the stout one and the head off the slim one. It would take professional upholsterers weeks to clean the blood off the good dining-room carpet. But it didn't care. Its perforated stomach rumbled so loudly that the stout one said, "Is that thunder?" The slender one said, "A shadow falls across this patch of room; does a storm cloud advance upon us?" Oh yes, a hungry cloud of grotesque and unappeasable appetite advances, Local League ladies, a cloud eager to have its lunch.

"That the daughter is missing is not a good sign."

"And all these novels. One didn't notice a single book of etiquette among them."

"Well, well." Tufted Plum looked disappointed. "Our Mrs. Mott seems a bit out of her depth."

"Yes," said Anemic Giraffe, "one would have to agree, but then, Mary Lavinia, so are we."

Mary Lavinia Tufted Plum raised an eyebrow. "Do go on, Felicity."

Felicity Anemic Giraffe continued. "It seems our Welcome Committee did not decide, in the end, to be all that welcoming to someone so persistently in the news, so prominent in her campaign to free her husband. They have made their feelings known by their absence." Anemic Giraffe indicated the many unused cups and saucers. "Perhaps, Mary Lavinia, it falls to us."

They both squared their shoulders in a ladylike way, and appeared more grimly welcoming than ever.

In came Mrs. Mott again, looking distressed. "I've checked the basement laundry and the yard near the creek bed. I'm so very sorry that Henrietta isn't here. Perhaps we should gulp down our tea so I can go look for her.

Though I try to let her have the free rein a young girl needs, under the circumstances I'm still skittish."

Henrietta sighed and neatly pressed the blue velvet ribbon back down along the front of her dress. Then with as much grace as the movement would allow she crawled out from under the dining-room table, bringing *Chiller Thriller 14: The Thing That Lasts* with her.

"Henrietta!" said her mother. She looked relieved and horrified at the same time.

"How remarkable." The tone of Tufted Plum was distasteful.

"How lucky that it is only we who are here to witness an unorthodox entrance." The tone was similar.

"How do you do?" said Henrietta.

"Very well indeed."

"How nice of you to . . . emerge."

"I'm sorry to be late," said Henrietta. "I got lost in my book."

"What are you reading?"

"Do you care to read a bit of it to us?"

Henrietta curled her hands around the covers so that the Local League ladies couldn't see the artist's vivid picture of the Thing That Lasts on the front cover or the blood-dripping letters that said "Lunchtime!" on the back. "I'm rather shy at reading aloud," she said.

Despite herself, Mrs. Mott raised an eyebrow. *Shy* was one thing that Henrietta Mott was most definitely not.

"Oh, do, please." Tufted Plum clasped her hands together, clapping up a ghost of lavender talcum.

"It might amuse one." Anemic Giraffe tried to appear encouraging but only succeeded in looking as if she were approaching the early stages of a thrombosis.

"Well," said Henrietta, "if you insist."

Good, thought the Thing That Lasts. Distract them for a moment while I coil my muscles around my limbs and make ready to spring for the kill.

Henrietta opened the book. She saw her mother blanch.

My mother needs these companions, terrible as they seem, as much as I need her, thought Henrietta. And I already let her down once by being late and by hiding. I don't want to let her down twice in one day.

Henrietta looked down at the page and spoke.

"Then Glorietta Sweetpea swept the path in front of the little cottage. Very shortly her animal friends would arrive for tea, and all must be ready. The napkins folded on the table. The flowers set in fresh water in a blue vase. And the crumpets arranged in a wicker basket. How lovely! Buster Bunny, Sissy Squirrel, and Chuckie Chipmunk would have a wonderful time. She hoped they would be on their best behavior. She knew *she* would be."

Tufted Plum smiled in mild surprise. Anemic Giraffe pursed her lips, but nodded.

The Thing That Lasts, its clacking finger bones poised to strike, paused in horror. It had never heard such dreadful

*prose. It nibbled one of its lips in distress until the lip fell off
on the lawn. Then it shrank back as the story continued.*

"Glorietta Sweetpea still had time to wait, so she sat down
in the sunlight and busied herself with some mending. Out of
the old socks she made potholders for the poor. Nothing
made her happier than being silent, calm, and useful."

*The Thing That Lasts backed off. It was distressed, moan-
ing softly to itself. Silent, calm, and useful were like swear
words to it. But as it retreated into the gloomy shade at the
bottom of the lawn, it consoled itself. There was always later.
It could always wait. After all—not for nothing was it called
the Thing That Lasts.*

"What a very useful novel, full of good intentions and
right thinking."

"I'm not much for novels, but this one does seem a cut
above."

"As we Local League ladies insist on being."

"As you will insist too, once we recommend you for a
vote, Mrs. Mott."

"Which, I daresay, we will do. And heartily."

"We may be a small delegation, but all the better. Our rec-
ommendation can be unanimous."

The Local League ladies smiled at Mrs. Mott. For an
instant they looked human and even a bit lonely themselves.
Mrs. Mott smiled back. Henrietta felt more than a little sick,

but she slid *Chiller Thriller 14: The Thing That Lasts* underneath the cushion of the chair on which she'd perched. Time enough for this later. If her mother was happy—or anyway, happier than she'd been—that was enough for Henrietta. She relaxed.

"Have the Local League ladies ever thought of sponsoring, say, an independent film festival?" Henrietta asked happily, slopping some tea for herself into a cup and shoveling in several heaping spoonfuls of sugar. "If so, I think I might be able to come up with an entry. I'd do my level best anyway. What do you think?"

WHAT'S A FELLOW TO DO?

Kathleen Karr

*W*AS THERE EVER SUCH PICKINGS?

Slim grinned to himself as he hugged his baggy overcoat around crammed pockets. Pockets within pockets in his vest and trousers. Pockets lining the lining of his long coat. All stuffed with the bounty from opening day of the fair–the Columbian Exposition of Chicago. Yes sir, 1893 was a great year to be alive, and this was a great day in May. Cool and cloudy it was, with brisk winds sweeping in from Lake Michigan. None amongst these surging crowds would question his need for the billowing coat, lumpy with the spoils of his trade.

Slim caught himself chuckling aloud. A hundred thousand people or more, their purses all his for the fifty cent admission. And them fair coppers! He snorted in derision.

Bunch of old codgers, the lot of 'em. Never seen such a lame crew. Didn't give a fellow half a challenge. Surely no challenge at all for Slim the Needle, the preeminent fourteen-year-old pickpocket in all of Chicago. Should he put 'em on their mettle one last time? Or should he head back to French Louie waiting for the haul outside the entrance gates?

Slim did most of his thinking with his body, and now his skinny, overgrown boy's form curled into the wind in a question mark. His pockets were full. Go or stay?

He was distracted by the vast white structure sitting before him by the Basin. What do you suppose a "Manufactures Building" might hold? His eyes darted around. French Louie never need know that he, Slim, had taken an hour or two holiday. Old Mother Hubbard was supposed to be working the buildings themselves for satchels and a little light shoplifting, but if he bumped into her, he could say he was casing the place. Checking it out for bigger and better things. Maybe that's what he *would* be doing. The question mark changed into an exclamation point topped by a gray felt hat, its brim pulled low over matching gray eyes. Gray all over and almost as transparent as a ghost, Slim dissolved through the crowds and into the building.

A figure nearly as transparent as Slim's made her way past the far side of the same building, trudging slowly, huddled against the wind. She was only a few years older than Slim, and equally skinny, but skinny from hunger, not growth. She was also burdened, though her load was hardly stuffed pockets. It was a bundle tightly wrapped in an old, coarse shawl. The bundle whimpered.

"Hush, darlin'. I'm doin' the best by you as ever I can."

Eyes darting even more warily than the pickpocket's, the young mother fearfully assayed the waiting entrance. At a break in the crowd, she crept in. Her eyes widened at the light, and the magnificence of the space opened before her under the endless, arching roof. Acres of space filled with machines and displays and exhibits—even castles—all beyond her knowing. She hugged the bundle more tightly.

"All these wondrous things," she whispered to it. "Rich folks' things. Rich folks' inventions. If the Lord has any mercy, there'll be a rich family coming by to care for you." She turned a corner round a machine and staggered on down a long aisle. "But it'll need to be the right place."

The frail figure stumbled on her way, lost in the maze of objects she'd never understand. Nearly in despair, a scent came to her. Her head rose. Perfume? Rich folks could afford perfume, fine French perfume. She pushed herself farther, following the aroma's trail. The booth was set off almost by itself in a corner. Glass cases were filled with lovely bottles. More bottles sat on open shelves, surrounded by a halo of subtle fragrances. It was the closest she and her child might ever get to heaven.

Her body made a sharp spin of surveillance. Blessedly no one, not a solitary soul, was nearby. She knelt as if to pray. Instead she opened the bundle long enough to kiss a soft forehead, to touch a silky blond curl, to gaze into trusting brown eyes.

"Forgive me, darlin'. But I'll always love you. Forever and ever. Your mama will always love you."

She crawled beneath the counter to tuck the bundle safely out of sight, then scurried from the overwhelming scent of rose and lavender. None among the boisterous crowd in the vast building noticed the running girl, tears streaming down her face. None but a young pickpocket on brief holiday. But he was quickly diverted by the spire of a colossal clock tower planted smack in the center of the building. As he stared up and up its 135-foot height, chimes began to strike the hour of three, reverberating throughout the building.

"*Criminey.*" Slim whistled with awe despite himself. "Now wouldn't that be a timepiece to go with a fellow's fob!"

In a forgotten corner of the building, a small hidden parcel began to cry softly, suddenly filled with all sorts of hungers.

Slim the Needle stopped in his tracks before the exhibit that had just caught his eye. No. It had caught more than that. It sent tingles through his spine. It caused every cell in his body to vibrate. He slipped between the gates of a gilded, eagle-tipped tower, to enter the realm of paradise.

"Tiffany's," he breathed. "This is *Tiffany's.*"

The contents of the display cases surrounding him almost overcame the boy: six-shooters with richly graven silver handles; heavily ornamented silver tea sets; loving cups,

bonbon boxes and tankards of gold. What couldn't he do
with such loot! He could get out from under French Louie's
thumbscrews, find his own fence and set up in business for
himself. Clover. He'd be in clover forever.

"*Ooob,*" he crooned softly. The tingles reached the hum-
ming cells of his fingertips. They grasped convulsively of their
own accord. "Come to Papa. Come to Slim."

Lost in his dream, Slim totally ignored the hovering
guards and swept on to the center of the display. Here were
glass cases stuffed with diamonds and pearls. His entire body
palpitated before a velvet pyramid revolving slowly on a
golden pivot. Inset against the velvet, flashing fire, was a jewel
the size of a walnut, a jewel the likes of which he could never
have imagined. The tiaras and necklaces and bracelets surrounding this gem dimmed to nothingness. Slim mouthed
the inscription mounted beneath. "The Gray Canary
Diamond . . . Lord," he reverently intoned, "but such a tiepin
that'd make!"

His brain began to grind at top speed. His eyes did their
part too. Figure the dimensions of the case. Estimate the best
spot to broach it. It wouldn't be the same as picking a pocket,
that was sure. This was something far grander; grand theft, in
fact. Was it possible, or only a pipe dream?

"You, there!"

"What?" Slim skipped back a pace at the sharp bark, automatically hugging his jacket and its hidden pockets to his
body, automatically closing off his thoughts, too, as if they
could be read.

"Stop breathing on the glass! You're fogging it up." The guard whipped out a handkerchief and ran it lightly over the smooth surface. "Put too much pressure on this here case and the alarms'll go off," the man continued to grumble. "And they sound like the very end of the world."

"Sorry," Slim muttered. He backed farther away. Then, still so overwhelmed with shattering new ideas and emotions that he could digest no more, Slim stumbled from Tiffany's and wandered in a daze through the remaining acres of the building.

Tiffany's was an epiphany. In one crystal-clear moment it brought Slim's entire life before him. Good and bad. Mostly bad.

Yeah, so I'm a pickpocket, he growled to himself. *A thief.* Is that any reason for the entire world to scorn me? To treat me like the scum of the earth? It's a profession, like any other. A skilled profession. It requires timing, and daring, and courage, too.

And it's not as if I prey on just anyone. I've got my standards, after all. I'd never lighten the pockets of the poor slobs in my neighborhood—they none of them have more than a few pennies to rub together anyhow. Nope, it's the bigwigs I go after, the fat cats, the very important men with eight-inch cigars and rubies flashing on their pinkies. Sometimes their women, too. But only the ones who look down their noses at me and my kind, like to say we'll give them lice, or worse. A real lady I wouldn't ever touch, because *real* ladies are like flowers. They make the world blossom.

Slim shoved his hands deep into his pockets, unconsciously following a scent of flowers.

His mother's face flashed before him. His mother might've been down on her luck, but she was a real lady. Only trouble is, she was one of those delicate flowers. She faded early and fast, just the way his little sister had a year before, leaving him to his own resources. That's how he ended up with French Louie's gang. It was Old Mother Hubbard who'd found him wandering around the streets after the consumption finished off his ma and the authorities came and took away what was left of her.

Slim was six. His mother was proud of a lot of things, and one of them was his birthday. "Never you forget, Thomas." Her words came back—Thomas was his given name, but he'd never use it on the streets on account of it was still like a private gift from her. "Never you forget that you were born on the Fourth of July in the year 1878. That makes you even more of an American than most people. That's why I named you after one of our greatest presidents, Thomas Jefferson."

Thomas Jefferson James, Slim mused. *That's who I used to be. Who I might've been. Without the consumption and French Louie.*

Slim's nose tugged him through the crowds and around a corner. His legs kept moving down a new aisle.

Ain't whining, he tried to convince himself. He had a skilled profession. And Old Mother Hubbard always did like to cook. She and Black Lena and Kid Glove Rosey kept a big old house for French Louie and Hungry Joe and Grand Central Pete. They'd collected lots of other kids after him, and started up a real school. Taught us how to read with the Bible, he reminded himself. Right, so we could learn to choose marks out of the newspapers. Taught us arithmetic, too, so we could count up our pickings and divide them equably—after French Louie's cut. Taught us other things as well. Slim toted them up in his mind: sleight of hand, and how to disguise ourselves for a job, and how to melt into a crowd. Regular humanitarians, the lot of them.

Then you start to grow a little, and you turn fourteen, and you're not cute anymore. You wake up on your cot one morning and learn what's expected of you.

The games become a job like any other. A skilled profession.

Slim shook his head, bumping into a few easy marks without even noticing. But by then, something of it gets into your bones, maybe into your soul. Your fingers work on their own, and all your pockets fill up faster, and you see something like Tiffany's, and you begin to get bigger ideas. Ideas about cutting free, about independence, about why should French Louie keep getting a percentage when you're doing all the work?

Raising his head he finally, consciously, caught the scent he'd been following. *Perfume.* Hooking him by the nose, right down to the toes. His ma's scent. Maybe that's what'd been bringing her back. After trying to push her away for too long.

He followed the aroma like any ordinary sucker. Like Thomas Jefferson James, not Slim the Needle. What do you find at the end of the trail?

• • •

The far corner of the building was still empty, aside from escalating cries of bewilderment emanating from amongst the perfume display. Empty until Slim arrived, following his nose. Then the vision of Tiffany's all mixed up with his mother's face burst.

"Here now, something's amiss." Without thinking, he crawled under the counter and headed irrevocably toward the source of the noise. In a moment he was cradling the bundle and the yowls ceased. He poked through the shawl to find the curly blond head and big brown eyes. The creature smiled at him, and a smile of wonder crossed his own face.

A baby.

A baby who'd maybe be crawling around lost, if she could crawl yet. A baby who looked like the prettiest little flower ever created. Like his own lost sister.

"Hoy in there!" a huge voice roared. "What've you got in your arms?"

Slim stared up at the guard. He'd found her fair and square. The first thing he hadn't stolen since he was six. Someone who had smiled on him with no reservations. With love. The way his ma and baby sister used to smile on him.

"She's mine!"

He hugged the bundle to his chest. He knew how to read and write. He could start over with something better than cold, glistening jewels. Be Thomas Jefferson James. Make his ma proud.

"It's my baby sister. I was just changing her wrappers, private like."

"Move along then, when you're done."

"Yes, sir."

Slim grinned at the baby and figured they'd get along just fine. She was a natural thief too. She'd stolen his heart, hadn't she?

He shrugged.

What's a fellow to do?

WET HENS

Ellen Wittlinger

I AM SO MAD! JOLENE AND I HAD PLANNED TO RIDE DOWN TO THE BEACH IF IT WAS NICE TODAY BECAUSE IT'LL PROBABLY BE THE LAST HOT WEATHER FOR A while, but instead I'll be spending my beautiful Saturday alone because I'm definitely not speaking to Jolene again. Ever. Unless she apologizes. And Jolene *never* apologizes. My grandmother uses this funny expression "madder than a wet hen." I've never seen a wet hen since we live in the suburbs, and I don't think they even let you have live chickens around here, but I have seen a wet cat and they can get pretty darn mad, and I am madder than that!

The more I think about it, the more I don't know why Jolene and I were ever friends to begin with. It's our mothers' fault. Just because *they've* been friends since Columbus landed, they decided *we* had to be friends too. Which is dopey because we're not anything like our mothers. All they're interested in is growing roses without pesticides and getting the town to recycle tin cans. Oh, and making sure Jolene and I are inseparable—that's their mission in life.

It almost worked, too. I mean, even *I* thought we really were best friends. *Wrong.* A best friend would never turn on me the way Jolene did yesterday afternoon. It was after our rehearsal for the Tappin' Tootsies, this dance group we belong to. I know it sounds silly, but it's really fun; we've been doing it together since we were seven and now we're eleven so I guess we're about halfway through our Tootsie years. Although, maybe not. Maybe one of us will quit now because how can we be together four afternoons a week if we can't stand each other? Thank goodness there's no class today so I don't have to look at her!

What happened was, last week we auditioned for solo parts for our fall dance numbers. Ms. Kramer, our teacher, is very fair about solos; sooner or later everybody gets one. And Jolene and I are both pretty good, so we've each had a few solos over the years. But this year was going to be different because the Tappin' Tootsies weren't just putting on their show in front of the parents and grandparents and other assorted relatives who *had* to show up—we'd do that too—but this year Ms. Kramer also got us into a competition show the day after Thanksgiving in *Florida.* A place I've never even *been* before. And after the competition we're going to have a day at Disney World, too, which with all the Tootsies together will be such a blast. If I go.

The other thing I should tell you is that Danny Wexler joined the Tootsies this year. Danny Wexler is thirteen, but short. He just moved here from someplace out west and he already knows how to tap-dance. We don't get too many boys in the Tappin' Tootsies—maybe it's the name. There was one boy who was really good, but he turned sixteen this year which is too old to be a Tootsie. Anyway, you can imagine that Ms. Kramer is happy as a dry hen, or whatever, to have another boy in class. Now she can do some couples stuff with her one short boy. And it just so happens that I am also short. Jolene, however, is considering a career with the WNBA.

So, not only did I get picked to do a solo in one number, but I also got a duet with Danny Wexler in another one. Jolene just got chorus. And then she got wet-cat mad. Or, actually, what kind of animal gets jealous? Because that's what she really was—mean jealous. Jealous as a hen who can't lay any eggs when the hen next to her is popping them out like a gumball machine. Okay, that was gross.

Anyway, this obviously isn't *my* fault! I can't help it I'm shorter than she is. And probably a better dancer too, if you want to know the truth. When Ms. Kramer posted the list on the door at the end of class yesterday and Jolene saw the parts I got, she stomped out to her mother's car and started to *cry!* We followed her out and Jolene's mother congratulated me really loud, to cover up the boo-hoos—although I have to say *she* looked kind of grumpy too. Then Jolene yelled, "You always get everything, Karly!"

"I do not!" I said. "You won the geography bee." I still didn't get it that she was being a real brat, so I was trying to cheer her up.

"Oh, big deal. You got your picture in the paper last year!"

That was true. At last year's Tappin' Tootsies recital, a photographer from the local paper took some pictures and he just happened to get me tipping my silver top hat to the audience. I was so proud of that picture—I looked very professional. Mom cut it out and hung it on the refrigerator for ages. But is it my fault the photographer took my picture and not hers?

"Now, Jolene," her mother said. "Don't be a poor sport. You've had solos too."

"But not in Florida. Not for competition. Not with a *boy*!"

"It's not a solo if you dance *with* somebody," I said. "It's a duet." Jolene glared at me.

"You'll still get to go to Florida!" her mother said with a big fakey grin on her face.

My mother chimed in. "Karly and I are sorry you didn't get a bigger part this time, Jolene. I'm sure you will next time."

Jolene had stopped crying by then. "Karly isn't sorry. She likes it when she gets bigger parts than I do. And better grades, too. Karly's a teacher's pet. She's always gotta be the winner of *everything*." Her voice was just plain lowdown mean. It felt like she was banging me over the head with it.

"That's not true and you know it!" I hollered back.

"That's not true and you know it!" she said right back, mimicking me and making me sound really whiney. Now I felt like crying too, but I wasn't going to do it in front of Jolene while she was being so rotten.

The mothers pulled us apart then and hustled us into our own cars. They said a few words to each other to try to smooth things over, but they didn't sound much friendlier than we did.

The only thing Mom said to me on the drive home was, "I'm sure Jolene didn't mean those things she said. She was upset. She's probably sorry already." Then she turned the corner too short and ran the tire up over the curb which made her swear like, you know, something with wet feathers. (Being a feminist and all, she probably wouldn't appreciate being called a hen.) And that was the end of that conversation.

Jolene's mother called about an hour later and apologized to my mother, which made both of them feel that everything was just fine again. "Helen admitted she was feeling a little bad herself about Jolene's being slighted. She said she's sorry now she didn't intervene sooner to stop Jolene from saying those mean things to you."

"So what?" I said. "Just because her mother is sorry doesn't mean Jolene is. She's a lousy friend and I'm never speaking to her again."

"Karly, come on, you know Jolene's just envious of you. You *have* gotten more attention in dance class lately. Can't you be a little forgiving?" Mom gave me her stern look. "After all, Jolene is your oldest friend."

"Not unless she apologizes." Which I knew she'd never be able to do. Jolene can never admit she's wrong. I always have to be the one to make up with her after we argue. Well, this time I'm not going to do it. It's *not my fault!*

"Nobody's perfect, you know," Mom said. "It's not a good idea to judge people by their weakest moments."

"*Weakest?*" I said. "You call that weak? She was screaming at me!"

Mom shook her head. "Well, sleep on it tonight. Maybe you'll feel differently in the morning."

So now it's morning and I don't feel one bit different. The phone rang about eight o'clock and I jumped out of bed just in case it was for me, but when it wasn't, I knew it wasn't ever going to be. That bratty Jolene can just spend the rest of her life alone because I certainly don't ever intend to call *her.*

The only problem is, I don't like going down to the beach by myself. There are always lots of older kids there and sometimes boys whistle or make remarks at younger girls. If I'm with Jolene it's okay because she just sasses them back, or else we both turn our heads away like we don't even hear them. But you can't do that as well by yourself.

So I decide to just ride my bike around. Maybe I'll find somebody else to hang out with. Unfortunately Jolene and I spend so much time together, just the two of us, that we don't really have any other good friends. I guess I always thought we'd be best friends forever and never need anybody else. Thinking that we aren't anymore makes me feel sort of sick and I can't finish my granola, even though Mom cut up strawberries on top.

It's the middle of September and the weather is perfect for bike riding. Or swimming. Or just about anything outside. I guess it's perfect yard-sale weather too, because I pass three of them just going around our block. One of them is really huge, and it looks like there's lots of kid stuff in it. Since there's nothing much else to do I stop to see what they've got, making sure to leave my bike parked down on the sidewalk so nobody tries to buy it.

Sure enough there's a table full of kid junk—girl junk, it looks like. A bunch of games—Boggle, my favorite—and Barbie dolls and oh, that mosaic tile-maker kit I used to have. I loved that thing! Whoever owned this one took better care of hers than I did because most of the pieces are still inside. And there's a kid's loom like the one I have at my grandma's house! The more I look around I see that whoever this girl is, we like the same kinds of things. I wonder why I never met her?

I take a good look at the house—a big white porch wraps halfway around it and there's a little yappy dog in the window. Wait a minute—I know who lives here. I didn't recognize it at first with all the stuff in the driveway, but now I remember. That girl Elizabeth—Porter or Potter or Parker. Something like that. She went to our school in kindergarten and first grade but then her parents put her in that snooty private school in Brentham, two towns away from here. I used to see her outside sometimes when I was younger, but now I'm always in dance class. Even though she lives close to me, Jolene and I never tried to get to know her—we figured she'd think she was too good for us.

It's weird she has so many of the same toys and things I do. Except she's selling all of them. I guess when you go to a *private* school you outgrow stuff earlier.

Now that I'm thinking of it, Jolene and I saw her one time a few years ago. Our mothers had dragged us to the mall to get back-to-school clothes and Elizabeth was in the same store—only she wasn't whining and begging to go get lunch like we were. She was trying on a skirt and blouse, turning to look at all different sides of her chest and her behind, making sure she looked perfect. I remember Jolene and I laughing about it and our mothers getting angry at us. But, really, who wears stuff like that to school in fourth grade? And who calls herself *Elizabeth* anyway? How about Liz or Beth or something that doesn't take half an hour to say? And now here's all her stuff, Elizabeth Whatshername's personal stuff, strewn around on the front yard like piles of garbage.

Then I notice the box of books. There's something I might spend a few quarters on. Old Elizabeth's probably reading Shakespeare already so maybe she threw out something I'd like. Of course, she has a lot of the same ones I do, but then I notice *it* shoved into the box sideways—my very favorite book from when I was really little, the one I made Mom check out of the library every few weeks and read to me over and over and over.

Carefully I lift the book out as if it might crumble in my hands. I have to sit down on the grass immediately and read it again. It's the story of a group of kids who find a hill in their town littered with old boxes and glass and rocks and they turn it into a pretend town of their own where they play for years. They called the town Roxaboxen and it always seemed to me like it must have been the best place to play in the world. They had a mayor and a graveyard and a bakery. And they had wars—boys against the girls—and a jail, and cars. I used to force Jolene to help me make a Roxaboxen in my backyard, but she was never into it the way I was. Anyway, you'd need a whole lot of kids to make a whole town. But at least now I have the book—I can read it whenever I want!

"Have you read that book before?" The voice behind me makes me jump. It's Elizabeth, of course, in a pair of ironed jeans and a tucked-in white shirt.

"Thousands of times," I say, hugging it to my chest. "I'll buy it from you."

"You can have it if you like it. I have another copy inside— I got two for my birthday one year."

"Are you keeping the other one?"

"Oh, yes. It's my favorite picture book."

I get to my feet, amazed. "It's mine, too!"

Elizabeth nods. "I thought it might be. I used to watch you and Jolene making the house markings with rocks in your backyard."

For a moment I just stare at her. She used to watch us playing? "Why did you watch us?"

She shrugs and sticks her hands in her back pockets. "I didn't know you well enough to go over. And there aren't any kids from my school around here so I never had anybody to play with unless my mother arranged something. Anyway, it was fun to watch you guys—from up here on the hill I could see into your backyard pretty well."

I take a look—sure enough, there's my badminton net, the tea roses by the barbecue pit, my cat, Weed, stalking into the tomato patch. I'm very surprised to be standing here talking to Elizabeth Parker-Potter-Porter who likes all the same things I like. When she smiles at me she doesn't seem snotty at all.

"I always wished I had a best friend like you and Jolene did."

I don't know what to say to that, so I grin and change the subject. "We saw you once, in a store with your mother." That's brilliant. Who cares? She'll never remember it anyway, but it's the only thing I can think of to say.

Elizabeth blushes a bright, hot red. "I remember that. I was so embarrassed you guys saw me in those dumb clothes. We have to wear matching skirts and blouses to school every day—otherwise I'd never pick out anything that dorky. I wanted to disappear—I thought you guys were laughing at me. . . ."

Now I think *I'm* blushing. "Us? No! We weren't laughing at you. Jolene just . . . told me this really funny joke, is all. I'm pretty sure that's why we were laughing."

Elizabeth sighs. "That's good. Sometimes people make fun of private-school kids. Like it's *our* fault we have to go there. I'd rather just stay in town and go to public school like everybody else."

"You would? Do your parents make you go to Brentham?"

She nods. "They think I'll get into a better college if I go to private school. I don't even think that's true, and, anyway, I don't care."

"That stinks," I say.

"Yeah."

"So how come you're selling all your stuff?"

She sighs again. "We're moving to California in three days."

"You *are*? That's so cool! You're so lucky!"

Elizabeth makes a face. "You think so? I don't want to move. I won't know anybody there."

"Yeah, but you'll be in California! No winter! No snow!"

"I like snow," she says.

I have to laugh. "Actually, so do I."

Elizabeth laughs too. She seems like such a cool person, I can't believe I never got to know her all these years. She's so much more like me than Jolene is.

"Hey, do you want to go to the beach? Maybe we could build sort of a beach-type Roxaboxen," I say.

Her eyes get big and round. "Yeah! That's a great idea. There won't be boxes, but there'll be rocks and shells."

"And driftwood . . ."

"And seaweed!"

I'm inspired by the fact that she thinks I have great ideas and I say, "We can call it Shellanroxen!"

She jumps in the air. "Yeah! Oh, Karly, let's!"

"I'll go get my suit and be back in five minutes," I say, running toward my bike, my favorite book under my arm. As I pedal past the house I see Elizabeth leaping up the stairs into her big white house, someone who seems happy to be my friend.

We spend a long time at the beach. Elizabeth brings a thermos of lemonade and some apples. I make off with a box of cookies from our cupboard so we have a good lunch. And we each have a dollar to get something from the ice cream truck when it comes around. Building Shellanroxen makes us act silly, like littler kids than we are. We make about six "houses" in the sand and then pretend to be different people depending on which house we're in.

"I know," Elizabeth says. "I'll pretend to be Jolene!"

"No!" I say, remembering how she glared at me yesterday. "Let me be Jolene."

"Okay then, I'll be you. I'll be Karly."

I laugh. "Then I'll have to come to your house—Jolene never likes to play at her own place."

Elizabeth straightens her beach towel (bed), leans against the rock (back wall) of her house and waits for "Jolene" to arrive. I arrange my face in a pout and shuffle through the sand to her doorway, pretend to knock. "Karly" throws open the door and says, "Hi, Jolene! Come in!"

When I walk in she raises her hand in the air and I know what she wants to do. She must have seen Jolene and me do it in my backyard. "Do you know how?" I ask.

"Sure I do, Jolene. We made it up together, remember?"

Okay. We slap a high five with our right hands, bring our left feet behind our right legs and slap them too, then go into a shuffle-ball-step the Tootsies use all the time and end with a face-to-face double hand slap. Elizabeth is giggling like crazy—she's so happy she did it right, I guess. But it seems funny to me to do the slap-greeting with somebody besides Jolene. And even funnier that Elizabeth must have learned it from *watching* us all these years.

"What do you want to do today?" she says.

I try to act like yesterday's Jolene. "I want to be voted the mayor of Shellanroxen," I say.

"Okay," she says. "Since I'm the only other resident of Shellanroxen, and, of course, I vote for you, I pronounce you Mayor! Congratulations!"

"Good."

"*Now* what should we do?"

"Who cares. We'll just end up doing what *you* want to do anyway."

Elizabeth looks perplexed. "No we won't. You're my best friend, Jolene. We'll do whatever you want to do."

This is weird. "Then let's go into your room and look at your magazines," I say, since this is about all Jolene ever wants to do lately. She's into stuff like *Haircuts that suit your face shape* and *How to get rid of the worst zits.*

The real me usually puts up an argument, but Elizabeth/Karly says, "Great. I just got some new ones." We lie down on her towel/bed and she hands me a wad of seaweed. "This one has an article on long skirts versus short," she says. "Or would you rather read about Sarah Michelle Gellar?" We pull the seaweed apart as if it were pages until pretty soon we have a slimy mess on the stomachs of our bathing suits.

"Are you thirsty?" Elizabeth/Karly asks me. "I'll go get you some lemonade. Or would you rather have something to eat?"

I sit up and turn back into myself. "This isn't really working," I said.

Elizabeth's smile collapses. "Why not? I'm having fun."

"Well, you're being too *nice* to me. I mean, Jolene and I aren't so polite and everything."

"But you're best friends . . ."

"Yeah, but that just means we act like ourselves when we're together. Sometimes we even act . . . kind of mean."

"You want me to be mean to you?" she says.

"No. I guess I just want you to be you."

Elizabeth nods, but I'm not sure she gets it. I suggest we go swimming for a while, as ourselves, and get the seaweed rinsed off our suits. Elizabeth is a good swimmer and she wants to keep having races, but I get tired before she does. I keep thinking if Jolene were here we'd be dropping rocks about six feet down and diving to see who could find them first.

Finally it's getting late so we decide to pick up all our Shellanroxen materials and hide them behind a big rock in case we want to use them again. It's been a good day—there weren't even any older boys at the beach to make fun of us. To tell you the truth, it's one of the best days I've had all summer.

When we pull up to Elizabeth's driveway again, the yard sale is all cleaned up and there's a pile of trash at the curb. We lean on our bikes for a minute, and I think about what a good day I've had without Jolene. But I also think about how she would have liked the seaweed magazines and racing with Elizabeth. Jolene is a very good swimmer.

"Maybe we can do something tomorrow," I say.

Elizabeth spins her bike pedal and looks away. "I don't know. My mom says I have to help pack my things tomorrow. There's only a few days left."

How could I have forgotten that? Here I just found the perfect new friend and she's moving in three days! It isn't fair! "Oh! I wish you'd come over when you saw us playing in my yard," I tell her. "Then we could have had fun together *longer*."

"I guess I was afraid to, but now I wish I had." The corners of her mouth are droopy. "Would you tell me one thing before you go home, and tell me honestly?"

"Of course I will," I say.

"That day you and Jolene saw me at the mall—were you really laughing at a joke, or were you laughing at me?"

My voice gets caught down low in my throat. "Why . . . why would we laugh at you?" It had seemed okay to laugh at her at the time—she thought she was so special—at least that's what we figured. Our laughter couldn't hurt her—it could only make us feel better.

"You know—because of the prep school thing. I was so mad when I thought you were laughing at me."

As a wet hen, I think, but don't say it. Ugh. How can I admit to being so mean? Elizabeth will hate me forever. The only thing to do is . . . "I swear," I lie, "we were just laughing at a dumb joke."

She smiles. "Okay. I believe you. Listen, maybe I could come over for a little while tomorrow. Maybe I could meet Jolene too, before I leave."

That'll never happen. "Sure, if she comes over," I say.

"You could ask her to come over," Elizabeth says quietly.

Could I? "How come you're so interested in Jolene?" I ask.

She shrugs. "I've watched you for so long–it seems like the two of you belong together. It would be nice to know you both."

"Yeah, I guess," I say, nodding. "Maybe I could ask her."

Elizabeth waves as she rides up her driveway and disappears around the back of the house. I coast down the hill to my house, in no big hurry to get there. Fortunately Mom is outside petting her rose bushes so I have some privacy. Just me and the phone.

I still think I shouldn't have to be the one to do this. But something tells me I have no choice. I guess sometimes even if something isn't your fault, you have to get over it. Especially if the two of you belong together.

"Hi, Jolene?"

"Karly?" Her voice is soft.

"Yeah. I'm sorry about the argument yesterday." I don't say: *Even though I didn't start it. Even though you weren't fair and you mimicked me.* "I do wish you'd gotten a better part," I say, and that's the truth.

"I know," she says.

"You're just as good a dancer as I am. It's not fair."

"Yeah. Anyway, I'm glad you called. I've had a rotten day. I left my library book at school, I've already read all my magazines, and the cable is out on our TV. There's *nothing* to do!"

"Can you come over tomorrow? I want you to meet somebody."

"Are you kidding?" She sounds happy again now. "I'll go *anywhere*, do *anything*, to get out of this house! Who am I meeting?"

"It's a surprise," I say.

She squeals. "Yes! I love surprises!"

"Me, too. And I think you'll like this one."

For a minute she's silent. "Karly, thanks for calling me. I . . . you know . . . I was just so *mad* yesterday."

"I know," I say, smiling into the phone. It's not an apology, but it's close enough.

THE GOOD DEED

Marion Dane Bauer

Miss Benson was my good deed for the summer. Every girl in our scout troop was assigned someone. My friend Melody had Mr. Stengle. He's the oldest resident of the Riverview Nursing Home. He must be at least one hundred and two. He used to be a farmer, and all he ever talks about is the weather. Anne Marie got Mrs. Mechlenburg. Mrs. Mechlenburg has four children, all under five, and kind of bewildered, cocker spaniel eyes. Like maybe she doesn't know how they all got there. But I was assigned Miss Benson.

Miss Benson is old. Not old like Mr. Stengle, but old enough. And she's blind. "Sight impaired, Heather," our scout leader said. But whether you say "sight impaired" or "blind," the truth is, Miss Benson can't see a thing.

"What do I do?" I asked. "What do I say?"

"Start with 'hello,'" our scout leader said, like that was some kind of help. Then she added, "She's a retired teacher. I'll bet she'd just love it if you'd read to her." And she was off talking to Anne Marie about diapers.

The problem was I'd never been alone with a blind person before. Come to think of it, I don't suppose I'd ever even met one. And the thought of trying to talk to Miss Benson kind of scared me. Melody and Anne Marie and I all had the same number of badges though, the most of anyone in the troop, and I wasn't about to let either of them get ahead of me. So the next day I called Miss Benson—she sounded normal enough on the phone—then I set out to meet her.

Her place wasn't hard to find. She lived in the apartment building right next to the Piggly Wiggly, only a few blocks from my house. Which meant I got there really fast. Too fast. Then I kind of stood in front of her door, waiting, though I couldn't have said what I was waiting for. To figure out what I was going to say, I guess. After "hello," I mean. But before I even got around to knocking, the door across the hall from Miss Benson's apartment popped open and this girl I'd never seen before stuck her head out.

"What do you want?" she said, like it was her door I was standing in front of.

"I'm visiting Miss Benson," I told her, which was perfectly obvious.

The girl had long brown hair. Kind of a reddish brown. But it was a tangled mess. I'll swear she'd pulled it into a ponytail that morning without ever passing it by a brush. "Why are you visiting her?" she wanted to know.

It would have sounded really dumb to say, "Because I'm a Girl Scout, and she's my good deed for the summer." So I said instead, "I've come to read to her." And then I added, just in case this girl didn't know anything at all, "She's sight impaired, you know."

"No, she's not," the girl answered, with a toss of that tangled hair. "I've seen her. She's blind as a bat."

Behind the girl, from inside her apartment, a whole lot of noise was going on. It sounded like the beginnings of World War III. Or like a herd of runaway horses maybe. Just then two little kids came hurtling up to the doorway and stopped to peer out from each side of the girl. I couldn't tell whether they were boys or girls or one of each. They looked kind of generic. Is that the word? Their hair wasn't combed either, and their noses were snotty. Great yellow gobs of the stuff ran right down to the tops of their lips. Their lips and chins were relatively clean, so I suppose their tongues took care of it from there. I decided maybe reading to a blind woman wasn't so bad after all and turned to knock on the door.

"Wait," the girl said. "I'll come with you."

Just like that she said it, as though she'd been invited.

And the truth was, I didn't know whether to be annoyed at her for being so pushy or relieved that I didn't have to go in there alone. What if a good deed didn't count if you had help? But though there wasn't a reason in the world for me to do what that girl said, I found myself standing there with my hand in the air, waiting.

"Tell Mama I've gone across the hall," the girl told the two snotty-nosed kids. And she stepped out and closed the door behind herself.

"Mama," I heard the kids yodel as they stampeded back into the apartment. And then there was nothing left to do but to knock on Miss Benson's door.

The rest wasn't nearly as hard as I'd expected. After a moment a tall woman with curly, salt-and-pepper hair opened the door and said, "You must be Heather. Come in." I could tell she couldn't see me, because she looked right over my head like there was something interesting on the wall across the way, but her voice didn't *sound* blind.

I don't know what I mean by that exactly, except that she didn't sound like she was missing anything at all. And I guess she wasn't, because when the girl said, "Hi!" and followed me into the apartment Miss Benson asked right away, "Who's your friend?"

Of course, I didn't have a clue who my "friend" was, but she answered, just as pert as you please, "Risa. My mom and me and my little brothers"—so they *were* boys—"just moved in across the hall."

"Welcome, Risa," Miss Benson replied. Her voice sort of had a smile in it. "I'm glad to see you."

Just like that she said it. *I'm glad to see you!* Like she could.

Miss Benson led the way, one hand trailing lightly across the furniture she passed or sometimes just grazing the wall. "I hope you don't mind if we go to the kitchen," she called back. "It's the cheeriest place."

The kitchen was a cheery place. The sun was all spread out across a table made out of some kind of golden wood. And in the middle of the table, sweating coolness, sat a pitcher of lemonade and a big blue plate heaped with oatmeal-raisin cookies. There were glasses, too. Just two of them though.

"Mmmm, cookies," Risa said.

"Help yourselves, girls," Miss Benson told us. "I made them for you." And it was a good thing she extended the invitation, because Risa already had one in her hand.

Miss Benson went to the cupboard and got out another glass and began to pour lemonade for everyone. She stopped pouring before she overflowed the glasses too, though I couldn't figure how she did it.

I expected Risa to gobble her cookie, just the way she had grabbed it off the plate without being invited, but she didn't. She just took a couple of nibbles, then tucked the rest into the pocket of her cutoffs. Can you imagine that? An oatmeal cookie in your pocket?

"Tell me about yourselves, girls," Miss Benson said, sitting across from us at the table, and before I could even open my mouth, Risa was off and running.

She told about her three little brothers—there was a baby I hadn't seen; he probably had a snotty nose too—and about how her mom had moved to Minnesota for a better job, only Risa didn't like her mom's new job because the boss wouldn't even let her take telephone calls from her children when she was at work.

I told Miss Benson how many badges I'd earned and how my parents and I had gone to Disney World over spring break. I could tell, just by the way Risa looked at me, that she'd never been near any place like Disney World and that she hated me for saying I'd been there. But what was I supposed to do? It was the truth.

When Miss Benson pushed the cookies toward us and said "Help yourself" again, quick as a flash, Risa took another cookie and put that one into her pocket too. I figured she must be stashing them for the snotty-nosed brothers at home, and I was almost impressed. It was kind of nice of her, really, to think of her brothers that way. It made me wish I had a little brother or sister to take cookies home for, but if I had one, I'd teach mine how to use a tissue.

And then I offered to read, so Miss Benson sent me to her bedroom to check out her bookshelf. I found a tall blue book—it looked kind of tattered, so I figured it had been around awhile and was, maybe, a favorite—called *Stories That Never Grow Old.* There was a picture on the cover of a woman wearing a long dress reading a book to some children.

When I came back with the book, Risa looked at it and said low, under her breath, "Dummy. That one's for little kids."

I shrugged, like I didn't care, but still my cheeks went hot when I opened it and saw she was right. It was a lot of old-timey stories like "The Little Engine That Could" and "Hansel and Gretel" and "Why the Bear Has a Stumpy Tail," things like that. Probably not what a grown-up, even one who used to be a teacher, would want to hear.

But then Miss Benson asked, "What book did you get?" and when I told her, she clapped her hands and said, "Perfect!" So I shot Risa a look and started to read. "'Bruin, the young brown bear, was feeling very hungry.'"

Risa leaned across the corner of the table so she could see the page too. She even started silently shaping the words with her mouth as I read, like she was tasting each one. I figured she must not be a very good reader though, because I'd given up reading with my lips when I was in the first grade.

As soon as I'd finished the story I knew I was right about her not being a good reader, because Miss Benson said, "Okay, Risa. Why don't you read the next one?"

While I was reading, she couldn't get close enough to the book, but suddenly she couldn't get away from it fast enough. "Oh no!" she said, pushing away from the table so hard that her chair screeched against the floor. "Anyway, you don't want to hear any more from that old thing. I'll do something else for you instead."

Miss Benson's face was round and soft. "What do you want to do instead?" she asked, and she folded her hands in her lap, waiting.

For a moment Risa looked around, whipping that tangled ponytail back and forth like she was expecting to find an idea for something she could do hanging on the wall. Then it must have come to her, because her face lit up and she settled back in her chair. "How about," she said, "if I give you an eye bouquet."

"An eye bouquet?" The way Miss Benson leaned forward you could tell she was expecting something grand.

An eye bouquet? I thought. *How dumb!*

But Risa explained. "I'll make a picture for you with words."

"What a wonderful idea!" Miss Benson said.

And it was a wonderful idea. I wished I'd thought of something half as wonderful. Though Miss Benson seemed to like the story I'd read well enough.

Risa thought for a few seconds, then she began. "The lilac bushes are blooming in front of the apartments."

Miss Benson nodded. "It's been years since I've seen those old lilac bushes, but they're still there, are they?"

"Yes," Risa said. "And they're that shimmery color, halfway between silver and purple. You know what I mean?"

"Shimmery. Halfway between silver and purple." Miss Benson nodded again. "That's it. That's it exactly. I can see them now."

I couldn't stand being bested by a girl who still read a little kiddy book with her lips, so I jumped in. I hadn't especially noticed the bushes she was talking about, but I'd seen lilac bushes all my life. "The leaves are shaped like little hearts," I said. "And they're green." I could see Miss Benson was waiting for something more, so I added, kind of feebly, "Green like grass."

But that wasn't any good, and I knew it. What could be more ordinary than "green like grass"? It's what my English teacher would call trite.

"The green of horses munching," Risa said, offering the words up like a gift, and Miss Benson tipped her head back and laughed out loud.

"Well," I said, getting up so fast I had to catch my chair to keep it from tipping over. "I guess I'd better be going. My father"—I leaned heavily on the word since it was obvious Risa didn't have one of those—"told me he'd take me and my friends to the beach this weekend."

It wasn't a lie. Daddy was taking me and Melody and Anne Marie to the beach, but not until Sunday afternoon. This was Saturday.

Miss Benson stood up too. "Thank you, Heather," she said, "for the nice visit. I enjoyed it. I enjoyed it very much."

"I'll be back," I promised. "I'll come and read again on Monday." *By myself,* I wanted to add, but I said instead, "I'll put your book away before I go." And I carried it back to the bedroom.

When I got to the bookshelf, I stood looking at the empty space where the book had stood. *Risa lives right across the hall,* I was thinking. *What if she decides to come back on her own? Maybe she'll even decide to read to Miss Benson, and this is the book she'll want, one that doesn't have too many big words.*

And then there I was, looking around for some place to put the book where she wouldn't find it. After all, Miss Benson herself certainly wasn't going to be wanting to look at it again while I was gone.

The wastebasket next to the bookshelf, rectangular and deep and perfectly empty, was just the right size. I slipped the book inside. It would be safe there, waiting for me.

When I got to the door, Risa was there, standing beside Miss Benson. She had to go home too, she said, though I knew she didn't have plans for going anywhere special like the beach. But I said all the polite things you're supposed to say to someone you've just met, to her and to Miss Benson too, and I left. My good deed was done for the day.

On my way out of the apartment building, I couldn't help but notice. The blooms on the lilac bushes were a crisp brown, the color of tea. So the girl was a liar, too, besides being a poor reader.

A couple of days later when I came to visit Miss Benson again, I stopped in front of her door, half expecting Risa to pop out of the apartment across the hall. All seemed quiet over there this time except for cartoons blaring from a TV. I breathed a sigh of relief and knocked on Miss Benson's door.

This time the blue plate on the table held sugar cookies, creamy white, just beginning to be brown at the edges, and sparkling with sugar.

"I'll get a book," I said, after we had each eaten a cookie and sipped some cocoa, chatting about this and that. And I hurried off to Miss Benson's bedroom to get *Stories That Never Grow Old*.

Only the book wasn't there.

I looked in the wastebasket, of course. I even picked it up

and turned it upside down and shook it, as though something as big as a book could disappear. But the wastebasket was empty. Just the way it had been the first time I'd come into the room. I wondered, in fact, why Miss Benson had a wastebasket at all since she didn't seem to put anything into it.

Then I hurried to the shelf. Maybe Miss Benson had reached a hand into the basket and found it there and put it away herself. Or maybe someone who came and cleaned for her had discovered it. Now that I thought about it, a wastebasket was about the dumbest place in the world to hide a book.

The space left behind when I took *Stories That Never Grow Old* out, right between two fatter books—*A Literary History of England* and *The Oxford Companion to English Literature*—was still there, empty, accusing. *You did it!* the space said. *You've lost Miss Benson's book! Probably her favorite book in all the world.*

Did she empty her own wastebaskets? She wouldn't have been able to see what was in there. Or maybe somebody else emptied them for her and thought, seeing it there, that she meant to throw it away. My heart beat faster just thinking about the possibilities.

There was nothing else to do, so I picked out another book, a collection of poems by Robert Frost, and brought that out instead.

"I have some poems," I told Miss Benson, and before she had a chance to say whether she was disappointed that I hadn't brought the blue book, I opened the collection and began to read.

"'I'm going out to clean the pasture spring.'"

She settled back to listen, a small smile tipping the corners of her mouth, but though she looked perfectly happy, I couldn't get past feeling that maybe she'd rather have heard *Stories That Never Grow Old*.

I read several poems—I especially liked the one about the boy who died after cutting himself with a chainsaw; it was so sad—but I kept feeling this weight in the pit of my stomach. The blue book was gone. Miss Benson had probably had it since she was a little kid.

I guess I quit reading without even noticing I'd stopped, because the next thing I knew Miss Benson was saying, "How about an eye bouquet now? What can you make me see?"

Her asking took me by surprise, because I'd already proven on Saturday that "eye bouquets" weren't really my thing. When I didn't answer right away though, she said, "I'll give you one first."

"All right," I said, though I couldn't help wondering what kind of eye bouquet a blind woman could come up with.

"Freckles," she said, "and hair the color of pulled taffy. Green eyes, a misty green like the sea."

For a moment I just sat there, feeling dumb, until gradually what Miss Benson had said began to dawn. *I* had freckles, though I didn't like to think they were the first thing a person saw. And my hair . . . well, it's the color people like to call "dirty blond," though I always hated that description. I keep my hair as clean as anybody's. But if you were being real nice, you could say it's the color of pulled taffy. And my eyes? Were they green like the sea? (I guess that would be better than green like horses munching.)

And then slowly, gradually, the truth dawned. Miss Benson had gotten her eye bouquet from . . .

"Risa's been here," I said. It came out sounding like an accusation.

"Yes. She came Sunday afternoon. She's a very nice girl. I'm sure the two of you are going to be great friends."

I ignored that, about Risa's being a nice girl and about the two of us being friends, because an idea was rising in me like dinner on a rocking boat. Risa had been in Miss Benson's apartment since the last time I'd been there. The blue book was gone from the place where I'd hidden it. Risa had taken it. I already knew she was a liar. Now I knew she was a thief, too!

"Okay," I said, "I can give you an eye bouquet. Hair . . ." I was going to say *Hair that's never seen a brush,* but something stopped me. Instead I said, "Hair the color of chestnuts." I paused. That was pretty good. And Risa's hair was a nice reddish brown. "And eyes . . . eyes like little bits of sky." I didn't even know I'd noticed those things about Risa—what a rich color her hair was, tangled or not, and the brilliant blue of her eyes—until I'd named them, but even as I did, I was standing up.

"Sor . . . sorry," I said, stumbling over my feet and my tongue at the same time. "I'm afraid I've got to go. I mean, there's something I've got to do. But I'll be back. Tomorrow. I promise."

Miss Benson stood too. "Is your daddy taking you to the beach again?" she asked.

"No . . . no." I was backing toward the door. "Not today. He's working today. But"—I'd reached the front door—"he'll probably take us again next weekend."

"That's nice." Miss Benson had followed. "Come back anytime, dear. I like having you here."

Come back anytime! She wouldn't say that when she found out her book was missing. Then she would think I was the thief. Because I was the one who'd had the book last, wasn't I? She'd never think of suspecting Risa of stealing a book, Risa who'd refused to read, Risa with her pretty eye bouquets.

As soon as Miss Benson closed the door behind me, I stalked across the hall and knocked on Risa's door . . . hard. I could hear the television still, Road Runner cartoons, but no one answered. The girl was hiding from me!

I knocked again, harder, and when still no one came, I turned the handle. Surprised to find the door unlocked—some people are incredibly careless!—I opened it slowly and peeked in. Two pairs of sky-blue eyes stared back at me from the couch. Without taking his thumb out of his mouth, one of the little boys mumbled, "Who're you?"

"I'm a friend of Risa's," I lied. "Is she here?"

They stared at one another and then, without answering, turned back to the TV.

"Where's Risa?" I said more loudly.

The one who had talked before pulled his thumb out of

his mouth this time. "She took Andrew and went," he said. "She told us to sit right here." He gave me a warning look. "She told us not to let anybody in, and we're not supposed to talk to strangers."

I stepped closer. Who was Andrew? The baby, probably. And where was their mother? Was she going to come marching in, demanding to know what I was doing in her apartment bullying her little kids? Not likely. This was Monday. She must be working. And Risa was supposed to be here taking care of the little boys. Well, so much for counting on her for anything. "When will she be back?" I demanded to know, stepping closer. "She's got something of mine."

No answer, so I moved between the couch and the coyote zooming across the screen, facing down the two small, dirty-faced boys. And that's when I saw it. The tattered blue book lay on the couch between them, open to a picture of a cheerful train puffing up a steep hill.

I snatched up the book. "Where did you get this?"

"Risa give it to us," the talker replied. The other one just leaned over until he had almost toppled onto his side, trying to peer around me to see the TV. Maybe he didn't know how to talk.

"I'll bet she did," I said. I could have burst. That buttinski girl who thought she was so great was a thief. Just as I'd thought.

The voice came from the doorway behind me. "Miss Benson gave it to me, and I gave it to them." I whirled around to see Risa, standing there holding an armful of baby. He was asleep with a fat cheek pressed against her shoulder. Risa looked small under his weight.

"Miss Benson gave it to me," she said again, as though she knew I didn't believe her, "when I went over there on Sunday."

"Where did you find it?" I demanded to know.

"Why did you hide it?" she countered.

The question hung in the air. The instant she asked, I realized I couldn't answer. Why had I hidden the book anyway? Something about not wanting Risa to horn in on my good deed. Was that it?

I tried another attack. "How come you went off and left your little brothers? Something terrible could have—"

She interrupted. "Andrew was sick. His temperature got really high. I couldn't get hold of my mom, so I went looking for a doctor." As she said it, she kind of staggered, like she couldn't hold up that lump of a baby for another minute.

Suddenly I could see how scared she'd been, scared for the baby, scared to go off and leave her brothers, probably scared to walk into a strange doctor's office alone too. "Here," I said, moving toward her. "Let me take him. Is he going to be all right?"

When I lifted the baby away from her, I could feel how hot he was. And how heavy, too.

"Yeah." She rubbed her nose with the back of her hand. Had she been crying? "The doctor gave him a shot. And he called my mom too. Her boss didn't have any choice. He had to let the doctor talk to her. She's coming home real soon."

I walked over to the couch and laid the sleeping baby down beside the other two boys. His cheeks were bright red. I took a tissue out of my pocket and wiped his nose.

"I'll bet Miss Benson would have come over to watch the boys while you went looking for the doctor," I said. And for a moment we both stood there, considering the word *watch*.

Risa nodded. "I didn't think of that," she said softly. But then she lifted her chin and added, like it was what we were talking about still, "I found her book in the wastebasket."

"Did you tell her?"

Risa tossed her head. Her pretty chestnut hair had been brushed that morning, and it flowed with the movement like a horse's tail. "Of course not. What do you take me for?"

Something deep inside my chest loosened a bit.

"Miss Benson said if I read out loud to my brothers it will help me get better. Better at reading, I mean." As Risa said it, a slow blush touched her cheeks, made her ears flame, even reached the roots of her hair. And that's why I knew she was telling the truth. Never in a thousand years would she have admitted that she needed help with reading except as a way of letting me know she hadn't stolen the book. "I'm going to read to her sometimes too," she added.

"That's . . . that's really great," I stammered. And I knew it was. Really. "You'll be helping her, and she'll be helping you. A kind of a good deed both ways."

"A good deed?" Risa laughed. "Is that what you call it?"

"Risa," one of the boys interrupted, the one I'd thought couldn't talk, "would you read to us some more?"

She looked sideways at me, and I knew that it was me—snotty me—who'd kept her from reading out loud before. "Why don't we take turns reading to them?" I said. "That would be fun."

Risa considered my offer long and carefully. "Okay," she said at last. "Just so it doesn't count as a good deed."

"It doesn't," I said. "I promise."

BARCAROLE FOR PAPER AND BONES

M. T. Anderson

ON THE DAY THEY FOUND THE SHIP, THE SEA WAS STILL, WEIGHED DOWN BY FOG. THEY HAD SAILED OUT OF GLOUCESTER HARBOR FOR THE Georges Bank, where they would drop lines for cod. They lowered the smaller boats, the dories, from their sides, and two by two, fishermen drifted off into the white.

They put down their lines. They stayed close to the schooner that had brought them out. Fishermen are sometimes lost in the mist.

Mist has a sound. It is muffled and dry. It makes all other noises brittle. For the whole of that dark morning, the fishermen sat in their dories, rocking on the sea. They ate their lunches, blind to all but gray.

In the afternoon one of the dories came upon a black wall in the ocean. They called out, but there was no answer. It was a ship without motion. The dory rowed around it, hailing. The sails still flew, though they were limp. The rigging hung. It was a clipper ship, and the name was painted on the bow: *The Sea-Pope's Barcarole.* The figurehead was of a buxom woman with her mouth open in an O, as if she were screaming and the fog were her own damp exhalation.

The dory did not stay long. The men began rowing quickly back to their fishing schooner. They looked over their shoulders in fear, and showed their teeth.

Two hours later the schooner pulled out of the mist alongside the dead ship. A party of men boarded her, climbing on ropes up the side. Their boots were heavy on the planking. They held lanterns and spoke loudly. The captain ordered that they search. "Find the ship's log," he said.

The dead ship's ropes were coiled neatly on their capstans. The rigging was in good order. The sails had not been damaged. No one had lowered the quarterboats to flee, for the boats still hung on the davits, trim and unused.

The fog was so thick, the fishermen could not see the top of the mainmast. One of them said, "Something could well be up there, looking down." Everyone stopped and squinted, chins raised. When they walked on, they stepped gingerly. On the forward deck, someone had stopped in the middle of scrimshandering. The whittling knives were laid on the planks. The project was abandoned. Someone had been whittling a whale tooth into a little statue of a man eating something—a loaf of bread, a liver maybe. A rooster with wild eyes was on his shoulder, whispering secrets in his ear.

The jib sails floated above them, three triangles crowding the gloom.

Belowdecks, everything was in its place. The ship was completely deserted. There was no one. No prisoners. No corpses. No sign of a fight. They found the hammocks in good order. Coats were hung on hooks, as if some men still were sleeping. Their boots had tipped over under their berths. The floor was marked with chalk for games of ringtoss.

In the captain's cabin the spyglass rolled back and forth on the desk.

In the mess they found a pot still sitting on the stove. One of them approached it. He reached out and held his nose. He did not want to smell what lay inside. He lifted the lid.

He screamed and dropped it with a clatter.

They gathered about him. They asked what he had seen.

Not what he had seen, he said. What he had felt. The oatmeal was still warm.

It was then that they became particularly cautious. The captain sent men to check the bilge. He told them to bring him all written documents that they found. He warned them to stay on their guard.

It was only minutes when a man returned and said, "Captain, I have found a journal. It was left out, with a quill beside it."

The captain, whose name, by this time, I had heard was Lurvey, said, "Good. And I have found a letter. I think it clarifies things." I could hear Captain Lurvey shifting in the chair, and then he asked, "But what does the journal say?"

The man answered, "It's long. I haven't read it yet. I've turned through the pages. The situation seems complicated."

"Was it written by the captain?"

"No. The captain is mentioned."

"That is too bad. I would like to find the ship's log. Still. Let me hear it."

"I am fearful of what the oatmeal means."

"I do not like the oatmeal either. Read."

The mate read out passages to his captain, as they stood there in the ghost ship on the silent sea.

Apr. 24th. The spring wind is fine, and we move apace northeasterly. We shall gain Salem-town before the next month is out. The weather, so felicitous, has prompted merriment among us. Beeton plays New Orleans bump-and-strut songs on the mouth organ. Ralph Goodgy lost his arms some years ago to a kraken, but still he can strum his dulcimer like angels when his stockings are off. We sing of the beauty of Spanish ladies; McClune is enthusiastic about mules. We heave the lines in rhythm to the songs. We know many halyard shanties. We won't let little Nehemiah Snitter sing us his one about an orange sea slug. There are limits to your patience, when you're eating hardtack.

Apr. 27th. Everything fine. Wind strong, and at our backs. We have come from Suriname, laden with molasses. Easter is already a memory. McClune just found the eggs in his boots.

Apr. 31st. Today we spied a little boat. Two men and a mast. No sail. They were stranded. Their skiff was covered in chalk markings from bow to stern. Egyptian, maybe. The men waved and shouted.

We have brought them on board. They eat like sharks.

The captain's mate kept flipping through the journal. He said, "It makes less and less sense." He read out lines as he flipped from page to page:

We cannot stop the growths in the hold. They are long, like spikes. Beeton tried to scrape them off. Beeton says they sigh. Worse, they are warm . . .

Goodgy still insists that someone stood with him for the whole watch. He says that they spoke. They saw nothing remarkable in those hours, but I wonder . . .

. . . retarred the hull. We should not have let the magicians on board.

. . . signs of rebellion among the rest of the crew. McClune and me, we will not buckle. We are loyal to the last. The singing has got louder since this morning. The boards vibrate. We have tried throwing stones at it.

. . . and all the food is burnt, now. I keep finding the feathers in my mouth. Tonight when I sleep, I will stay awake, and keep guard. I would like to see whether some traitor puts them in my mouth, or whether they grow, like mushrooms.

The dancing on the deck went on all night. Beeton fired at all eight of them as they poured down the stairs. They were dressed for some kind of ball. The captain was on the floor and could do nothing but wave his fins. I have been holding onto the cabin roof for some time now. Mark my words: Cross me, and I will drop on you.

It is circling the ship so quickly.

Will I see Salem again . . . ?

"That is all?" asked Captain Lurvey.

"Just excerpts," said his mate. "I could read the rest. It makes little sense."

"No. I can't see our men being pleased about this."

"Funny kind of date. April thirty-first."

"I have found this letter," said Captain Lurvey. "I think it is somewhat clearer. I will read it in its entirety."

"Could I sit?" asked his mate.

I was uncomfortable under the bed, and I wished they would take McClune's letter somewhere else. I did not know how long I could lie still. My arms were starting to feel like oak paneling.

April 31st, 1856

Dear Hetty,

I should not have left you on Cape Ann. Never. I guess you likely hate me by now. I hope you did not wait long for me on the Dogtown moors. I packed off that morning on a clipper ship bound across the sea.

I would have married you. I guess that night before, I looked at you, and suddenly I saw that some day you would be a woman, and I would be a man, and I started to hear the bawling of infants, and you saying, "Would you get that, Ned?" and me saying, "I'm going out," and you saying, "It's the babies. Get the babies." And I smelled all the puke there would be and saw you getting big again and again and then your eyes getting rings around them and your hair getting like some sticks. I saw what I would look like with a potbelly and hair on my nose and balding. So I went away to sea, and I cannot be sorry in enough ways. I love you. When you hear bells ring on the Dogtown moors, in the evening, when we would meet there in the rocks and ruins—when you hear those distant chimes, think of me. I love you. I love you. Know it's me ringing across the sea, I love you, Hetty. I'm sorry. I'm sorry. I'm sorry. I thought that I was a man, and that a man couldn't be tied down.

We didn't see the pirates until they were on us. They had cannon. We let them board. Figured, what's the worst they'll do?

"We don't have any gold," said our First Mate.

"Gold," said the Pirate King. "Now that's funny. Do bakers knock people down in the streets,

looking for doughnuts? So why would I want gold? Do you think there are no more deserted islands with hidden chests? No more secret coves? Are you under the impression, sir, that 'X' no longer marks the spot?"

The Pirate King did not want any metal or treasure at all, as it transpired. He wanted instead a gruesome shipboard theater festival. He said, "I am of a somewhat classical bent. At the moment, I am particularly impressed by the plays of the antique Greeks. Call me crass, but I read them in translation. Are you thespians? You will be soon. You will act out for me and for my crew the tragedies of Sophocles and Euripedes. We will supply the weapons."

For days it has gone on. There are three plays a day. The pirates have posted guards throughout our ship. We only get the weapons with which, on stage, on deck, we are to stab each other, cloaks which we must slather with acids, golden brooches with which we have to pluck out our eyes. After each performance, they wash the deck of blood. The water drizzles from the rails, pink.

I have never seen men sob as they do when acting these roles. We are wrapped in sheets, weeping. Men beg for mercy rather than slay their friends. Some have chosen to die rather than to run through with swords a man who yesterday hauled ropes beside them. Stuttering their lines, men flip forward in the script to see how many pages they have left to live. We calculate how long each page takes to read. We translate pages into minutes.

Before they die, delivering a final soliloquy, men pause and shut their eyes to pray in between sentences. They want to remember their wives and sons and daughters. They don't want to be playing someone from ancient Greece. They want to remember the coast of Cape Ann. It is written on the page when they shall die. A paragraph. A sentence. Two words more, and there is a cue for the sword.

My darling, my darling, you and I shall not meet anymore.

After each performance, the deck is like a set strewn with the bodies of the dead. We are told to let them lie. The Pirate King applauds. Then he gives us notes. "More passion," he says. "You should have seen the crew of the H.M.S. CERTITUDE working their way through the ORESTEIA. Now those men had the fire in the belly."

You cannot imagine the atrocities that I have seen on this ship. Slaughter every day. And speeches, speeches we make weeping while our friends bleed to death beside us. We stand in the shadow of the grisly sets, the open mouths, the empty sockets. The Pirate King says that when the gray bodies are enough decayed, then he will start on comedies. He has a particular enthusiasm for the farces of William Congreve.

In the spring the bluets will grow again upon the Dogtown moors. Think of me when you walk there. Do not think of my end. Take a husband, and tell him my story on nights when the storm is blowing around the Cape. Tell your children, so someone will remember me.

Tomorrow we act out the story of Iphigenia. She was a girl who was sacrificed to the gods so *that winds would return and blow the Greek fleet to victory. She was stabbed. The Pirate King says this is one of the last tragedies our crew will act, and then whoever remains alive will try a few farces and be set free. I close my eyes. In my breast, I can see what you would have looked like on our wedding day. The simple dress. The circlet of white lilies around your brow.*

I am dressed tonight like you would have been—the gown, the flowers. I am crying so hard my rouge is running.

My darling. O, my darling.

I am Iphigenia.

Yours, my love, yours, yours,
Edward McClune

For a long time after Captain Lurvey finished reading, the two of them were silent. I had lain too long beneath the bed. Pains were skating up and down my back. My elbows were ground in the dust.

"It makes no sense," said the captain.

"The two stories," said his mate. "Nothing matches up."

"No," said the captain. He sighed. "We will search again tomorrow. I do not want to be here at night."

"It is the oatmeal."

"No one likes that oatmeal."

"I will gather the men," said his mate.

The captain said, "The ship's log is missing. And so is the steering compass. Gone."

They rose, and I heard them walk out of the cabin. For a

while, I waited. The footsteps clattered up onto deck. They were crawling over the side. The ship would be empty again.

Gradually, I pulled myself out of my hiding place. I had been there for hours.

I crawled toward the stove on all fours.

When things were finally over that awful night weeks before, I had hidden in the hidey-hole. I would not budge. I still could see their faces and the backs of their hands. I could still hear Beeton shouting his last few morsels at the end. McClune. McClune. I knew that they all were gone. I knew that I traveled now on a ghost ship. I knew I was alone.

It was dark in the hidey-hole. There was a chest there. I crouched on top of it. Nothing. Darkness. I would not budge. I did not trust the silence. Someone could be toying with me. They could be waiting outside the door. They could find the silence luxurious. It could be a pleasure to them.

I do not know how long I hid. I thought only of the strangeness of it. I thought of McClune's face. I had reached out my hands to him. He was the last one I saw.

The wind took the ship. The sails, I knew, were still unfurled. The hull creaked. We passed into a storm. I banged back and forth in the hidey-hole. I slipped on the trunk's curved lid. I pressed against the walls with my palms. I sang capstan shanties and halyard songs in a warbling voice, through my snot. I sang what we had sung on the way out. "Farewell and adieu to you, Spanish ladies." Now alone. Whimpering, "Farewell and adieu, you ladies of Spain." I heard things rumble in the depths of the boat. Something had come unmoored, and was rolling and splashing in the hold. And I croaked, "Then lay me in the deep brown sea, boys, lay in me the sea, heigh ho. I'll no more see fair Ipswich Bay, fair Ipswich Bay by evening."

On other days the ship was stable. Perhaps the sun was out. We may have passed land. Or maybe, for as far as a gull could have seen, nothing but blank gray, the sea, the ocean like a stone. I did not leave the hidey-hole. I did not want to see the boots beneath the hammocks. I didn't want to see the checkers on the board.

If there had been anyone on the ship, they would have found me. I knew this. I could picture the ship, sailing through the day beneath the clouds in near silence, except, on one empty deck, a sobbing, a wrenching sobbing that went on for hours behind a wall. I discovered the trunk was slippery. At some point I had vomited, and there was no place for it to run. Quickly it grew sticky. I had not eaten. I prayed. Why should I be delivered from terrible danger, delivered as if by a miracle, only to die slowly in the following days?

And so I stepped out. I opened the secret door, and tiptoed through the ship. The stillness was terrible. The spyglass rolled on the captain's desk. The pots swayed on their hooks above the stove. I saw the lines still coiled on the deck. The buckets filled with rainwater. The hammocks and cots where we had sat in the salad days, daring each other to eat wood and metal.

I walked the decks, and waited for rescue. In every moment of every day, I felt the terror and loneliness of the empty clipper ship like soup spilled scalding on the smoothness of my skin. My arm hair was always up on end. It was tiring to feel fear so long. So I slept well, sometimes for days. But when I woke, it was always with a start, as if when I sat up, I would see three cat-eyes watching me unblinking from the dark.

I could not navigate. I couldn't haul the halyards or change the rigging. It took whole teams of men. I was just a boy. There was enough food, though, that I knew I could live until I was found. I pictured arms lifting me from the ghost ship. I pictured my first glimpse of Boston, or Salem, or Gloucester Harbor, how it would look, Straitsmouth Island, then Eastern Point, Norman's Woe. The little town on the water. My mother lived north, up 'Squam way. I would go see her. Everywhere, there would be human arms, kind human arms, and they would be warm in fabric, and would take me up. I would tell them of my adventure. I would call it an adventure. I would see the salt marshes at evening, the light glinting purple in the wet sand. There would be no more silence. The gulls are always squawking there. When you are nearer land. They throw clams down on the flats.

I read the captain's log. He had stopped writing when things became too strange. I read his final entries.

Now I was captain. I took up the quill, and began to fill in the log.

I ate salt cod, and wrote in the captain's book. I wrote the story of what had happened.

When it came to writing of the final terror, I found I could not continue. I did not want others, drawing the log from the wreck of the ship some day, to know. I did not think it was fair that they should be able to pronounce the name of what had happened without having lived it, that they should be able to say simply, with satisfaction, "Ah. Here is the crux." That is how it struck me then. Nothing is simple. You cannot know some things without living them. If you want to know a man, do you cut open his torso and measure his guts, and take him limb from limb? If you dismember him and name his parts, you will never know him. The truth, it is like that too. For the truth to be preserved in wholeness, I had to destroy it utterly, so there could be no glib examination, no work upon its remains.

And that is why I finished the captain's log filled with a lie, and threw it overboard.

That is why I found other journals, and ended them all with other lies. Each one a new lie, so no one could ever know the truth. I wrote about portents: miraculous bands of fire in the sky; men in gold armor who swam beside the ship for hours; schools of speaking dolphins. I could not stop myself. I wrote letters from men I had known to wives and to girls I never would meet. I wrote my lies in diaries, in journals, on charts, in menus.

The days passed. I do not know how many. Light from the portholes slid across the cabin. There was nothing but the smell of wood and tar and cold dead fish. I slept with my head on the captain's desk. My shirt was still greasy with old vomit. When I was awake, I stared at the waves, or I wrote. I wrote for whole days. I talked about death, and the sweetness of life. I described the way flesh could be pierced and burned. I made up mythologies. I was pleased by how terrifying they became.

And yet, much of the joy was not in making up the ghastly stories, but in writing the accounts of the men on the ship before the disaster. It was my tribute. I wrote down my memories of them, the things I had liked about them, and which I missed now in the silence. I told the story of Ralph Goodgy and his dulcimer. I retold jokes that Ginty O'Grady had told around the table. I wrote about the handsomest man on board, Rafe Frantic, hero and swashbuckler, beloved of the ladies, possessed of a tapeworm that won prizes at the county fair. I described my friend McClune and recalled the times that we had gone ashore together. He was a man who made you feel there was always an adventure to be found over a wall. We walked the streets of Macao and Calcutta. I told and retold the last moment I'd seen him, each time differently, each time with more fondness.

One day I looked down, and discovered I had written what had really happened to him. I stood up and backed away from the desk. I put down the pen as if it were hot.

The next day I sat in the forecastle, huddled in a corner, sure that something was going to change.

And sometime later, in the afternoon, through the fog, I heard voices. I felt terror again. It was not long before they boarded. At first I hid because I thought they were the bodies of the dead. I thought my captain had returned to find me. I did not have time to reach the hidey-hole. I crawled beneath the captain's bunk. I left my oatmeal on the stove.

And that night, when they had slipped back to their schooner, and only a single guard paced up above, I went to my store of forgeries. I brought the rest of them out. Confessions, meditations, inventories, dockets, account books, nautical memoirs. And all that night, I wrote by the light of the moon. I wrote new stories that told of new catastrophes.

And in the morning, scouring the ship, they found them in bunks, in cubbies, in pockets, in hats, in bags, in pots. They found them.

Two days out, we passed a New Bedford whaler. That was the last human sign we saw. After that, the sea became blanker and blanker.

A week ago, we started to notice the water was thickening around us. We pulled it up in buckets, and it was like jam . . .

For days, the rushing sound grew louder. It was like a falls. There were cries from the crow's nest. One of the icebergs had disappeared. A Portuguese sailor started screaming chants to the Virgin Mary.

He had seen that we had reached the edge. . . .

They found them in blankets, in drawers, on tables.
Books laid open during the night. Notes folded into eighths.
A single word in blood. Verses of a mad sea chantey:

We heard the tapping on the hull,
The tapping all heard we
Like a man who thrashed for life
Beneath the cold salt sea.
The lonesome waves, the crying whales
Beneath the cold salt sea.

"There is no man beneath the boards,"
Our Captain told us right.
"Then why does he knock rhythms out
Upon the hull all night?
Then why does he knock rhythms out
And moan with fear and fright?"

We sent a man below the boat.
We fastened him with line.
We keelhauled him and told the man,
"Pray God, and you'll be fine."
But though he sought the source that day
There wasn't any sign.

The lonesome waves, the crying whales
Beneath the ocean cold.
The banging spread and grew instead
Throughout the bilge and hold. . . .

We saw the plume of the volcano on the 31st day of April. Shortly thereafter, we beheld a miracle: There were bodies swimming through the water, translucent, fringed with webbing.

. . . have hidden here beneath the table. The blood still runs down through the gratings. The madness has spread to the cabin boy. God preserve him. I heard him rush up the stairs, yelling, "I'll trump you, lads, and take the kitty! Can I join your feast?"

I do not expect to hear from him again. . . .

. . . Shadow noticed first by moonlight. Could not tell what body cast it . . . Next day. Shadow has persisted. It is perfectly circular, and travels always over the ship. Sky is blue. Cloudless. The shadow moves with us. The sea is empty of objects. We are alone with the shadow. We have dropped the sails. It stops. We have tacked mightily. It moves wherever we move.

Nothing casts it. It is getting larger, as if, while the days go by, an invisible object gets lower and lower, nearer the masts.

I fear a storm. Under the clouds, the shadow itself will be invisible, like broken glass shards drifting in water. We will not be able to see the edge.

I wrote and I wrote. I heard them read the passages out loud. They clambered up and down the decks. I was in the hidey-hole.

You will not find me, I thought. *But on one of those notes, I have written the truth. If you can guess which, I will come out of hiding. I will come out, if you can guess which one happened.*

It has been two days since we dredged up the crucifix. I watched it one night, and Beeton the next. Both of us now coming out in sores. They are small and red. Feel like we have been pinched. The Captain says there is no cause for alarm. . . .

Cook says he will prepare a special dish in celebration. He says it's called "Twenty Sea Sparrows." He'll make it tomorrow. Whatever he made us for supper tonight is sitting heavy. Not a man of us can keep his head up. Me, weary like I've been beat with a stone. McClune is snoring like a buffalo in love. Well, reckon I'll get some sleep. The Captain is sitting by the door, watching us all and smiling. He is playing solitaire. Singing lullabies. I'm exceeding weary. The cook is sharpening knives. . . .

No light will shine when held down inside the strange new hatchway. There is no sign of Beeton. We have called his name. Soon I will try and . . .

Their bodies pass by our hiding place across the planks, whispering and twiddling their fingers. . . .

. . . until the first pinnacle raised itself out of the sea . . .

. . . the phantoms. McClune was the first to go.

. . . McClune was the last to go . . .

. . . the kite strings taut . . .

. . . under the idol . . .

. . . his tail to the . . .

. . . their wings . . .

. . . the cove . . .

. . . vanishing . . .

For a day they puzzled over all the documents. They tried to piece together some story. They failed. They were no match for my conundrum. They are worried about getting their cod back to shore. They do not like the atmosphere of the ship. That is weak of them. After a time you learn to live with fear. It becomes a condition of the skin.

I am sitting smiling in my hidey-hole. When they are

gone I will clean the trunk of vomit. No one will ever find me. No one will understand.

Captain Lurvey is the last to leave. He walks through the abandoned chambers. I hold myself rigid against the wall. A few more moments and he will be gone.

He is standing by the gangway up to the deck.

Suddenly, a soft and urgent voice, he calls out, "Why don't you come out, boy?"

I am frozen. I listen.

"You could just come out. We'll take you home. I am sure you have a mother who misses you."

She would not understand the things I have seen.

"We will not be back," he says. "You will be alone again."

I do not know why. I start to turn the knob on the door.

He says, "We know the writing is yours, child. Your handwriting is everywhere. You are what, fifteen? Sixteen? Come home. We are going back to Gloucester Harbor. We'll be there in a day and a half. Come with us. Come home."

Receiving no answer, he says, "The fog has broken."

There is a silence. We both can hear something dripping. When he leaves I will convince myself it is a thing which comes back to find me, and I will live in fear of it.

In a burst, as fast as I can, I call out: *"Which-one-is-real?"*

He moves quickly toward me. I hold myself still. He would like to hear another answer from me. "Pardon?" he says. "Could you repeat the question?"

I am silent. He knows well what I have said.

He walks softly across the floor. "I don't know," he whispers. "That's why we need you. You are important to us. You have to tell us the true story. Show us how you made up the lies."

The fool. He is a fool. A grown man, unable to see past the lies of a child.

I will stay here with my mystery. I will not go back to be prodded, and asked questions, and have my story told with woodcuts. I will not have men from Harvard say, "It cannot be true. The boy is lying."

I will stay with my secret. I have become used to fear.

After a while he leaves. I wait until I hear the oar strokes in the water.

I will glide on in my clipper ship. Night will fall, and I will enjoy my sleeplessness again. I will write more stories of what happened.

I will take time to sharpen the truth through lies. I will tell it many ways. I will sail on through fog and evening toward some shore, or some shoal, or toward the part of the sea which always is on fire. Toward the sporting grounds of serpents. Toward the arctic. Toward the Nile. Toward China, or France. That is what I want. It is what I would like. I will be alone. That is how I like it, alone, on this ship. Hearing the noises. Seeing their faces. Waiting for something to return. That is exactly what I want.

I am alone at sea.

We left behind the hulk of the Sea-Pope's Barcarole. *There was nothing more to find. We should reach Gloucester by noon tomorrow.*

The men say there is no explanation for the pristine state of the ship. In particular, they have discussed the oatmeal.

It is a haunted ship; of that, there is no question. It is not just haunted by the survivor. I fear that whatever took the rest of the crew will return to it. I fear that it will sail forever on the surface of the sea. I do not know that time passes the same way around it as elsewhere.

We are all glad to get away.

I fear most of all for the figure that watched us leave. I did not call attention to him. I could not tell: He was waving. But was he waving good-bye and good riddance? Or was he, at the last moment, calling me back? Did he want to be seen? There was something that he yelled. The wind was strong though. Strong and cold for spring.

We have caught twenty-three barrels of cod near the Bank. We are fletching them right now, cutting off their heads, salting them below.

I will be happy to see Gloucester-town.

—May 32nd, 1856

CLEAN SWEEP

⁃⁃⁃⁃⁃⁃⁃⁃⁃⁃⁃⁃⁃⁃⁃⁃

Joan Bauer

"*H*AVE YOU EVER SEEN A DUST MITE?"

My mother always lowers her voice when she asks this; it adds to the emotional impact. Never in the five years since she's had the cleaning business has anyone ever said they've seen one. That's because the only people who have seen dust mites are scientists who put dust balls on slides and look at them under microscopes. Personally I have better things to do than look at minuscule animals who cause great torture among the allergic, but my mother has a photo of a dust mite blown up to ten gazillion times its size—she is holding it up now, as she always does in this part of her presentation—and the two women who sit on the floral couch before her gasp appropriately and shut their eyes, because dust mites, trust me, are butt ugly. Think *Invasion of the Body Snatchers* meets *The Hunchback of Notre Dame,* and you're just beginning to enter into the vileness of this creature.

"They're everywhere," Mom says to the women. "Under the bed, on the sheets, clinging to the blinds; hiding, waiting. And at Clean Sweep," she offers quietly, but dramatically, "we *kill* them for you. We hate them even more than you do. *This* is why we're in business."

The two women look at each other and say *yes,* they want the cleaning service to start immediately.

Mom tells them our price. One woman, as expected, says, "That sounds a little high." People are so cheap. Everyone wants quality, no one wants to pay for it. Here's the suburban dream—to hire great workers who are such meek morons that they don't have the guts to ask for a living wage.

This is not my mother's problem. She holds up the dust mite enlargement to make the point. "We cost more because we know where he and his army are hiding."

She used to say "we know where he and his friends are hiding," but "army" sounds more fierce, and when you are serious about eliminating dust, you'd better let everyone know it's war.

"Well . . . ," the other woman says, unsure.

Mom presses in. "We suggest two cleanings per week for one month to achieve total elimination. Then weekly cleanings should do, unless you have special needs."

Special needs in the cleaning world range from cleaning out attics to detoxification of teenage bedrooms. I am a specialist in cleaning rooms of kids who have just gone off to college. It takes nerves of steel. And I have them.

My brother Benjamin doesn't. To begin with, he's allergic to dust—bad news when the family business is dedicated to eliminating it. To end with, he's a devoted underachiever, in stark contrast to myself. And Benjamin knows how to get out of work—he could give seminars on this. He gets the perfect look of abject pain over his face, says he's not feeling too well, he's sorry, he doesn't want to be a *burden*. He talks about the pain moving across his back, down his leg, and into his ankle. Then he gets dizzy and has to sit down; lying down comes moments later after his face gets a little pale (I don't know how he does this) and his hand touches his forehead which, I swear, has small drops of sweat on it. Then he'll try to get up and help, but by this time, you feel like such a snake that a sick person is going to get sicker because of your insensitive demands that you say, no, you rest, I'll do it.

This is what he's done to me today, and I'm not in the mood for the game. He tells me, groaning, he'll *try* to make it to Mrs. Leonardo's today to help her pack up her attic, but he's not sure he can even sit. He's lying on the couch in misery saying if he can sit, he will try to stand, and if he attempts standing, he will attempt actual walking—Mrs. Leonardo's house being four houses down the street. I throw my book bag at him. Suggest he *crawl* to Mrs. Leonardo's house and he says, "Thanks, Katie. Just thanks." To which I reply, "Look, Benny Boy, I'm getting sick of carrying your weight around here. If you think I'm going to do your job and mine until I die, think again." Benjamin groans deep, turns off the light, closes his eyes and says his headache is cosmic and could I please go get him some Advil.

I don't get the Advil. It's a big bad world out there and he needs to find it out now, at fourteen. This is what big sisters are for.

So I'm basically crabby and bitter all day; taking it out on random people. After school I have mounds of homework. You wonder what teachers are thinking—I have three hundred pages of reading in three textbooks plus a paper due on Friday. Have you ever noticed that it takes a textbook dozens of pages to say what normal people can cover fast?

Example:

What was the full impact of World War II?

Clear-cut teenage answer: We won.

So I'm close to dying young from excessive homework, and I have to help Mrs. Leonardo clean out her attic. She is paying big bucks for this, and, believe me, my family needs the money.

Mrs. Leonardo wants people there on time and working like ants. Ants carry their weight on their backs and are thrilled as anything to be abused. But that is the insect world; I am not one of them. I'm not in the mood to sit with her in her dingy attic and lug tons of garbage down the stairs and listen to her stories of how her family deserted her. I know that sounds mean, but Mrs. Leonardo is a mean person. It's easy to see why she's alone. The big joke is that when her husband died, he had a big smile on his face in the casket that he'd never had in real life. The funeral director said they tried to wipe that grin off his face, but they couldn't do it.

So I'm on my knees in the dust, putting things in bags, while Mrs. Leonardo tells me about her selfish brother Horace who deserted her, and her uncaring, money-grubbing cousin Cynthia who backed out of the driveway eight years ago and never came back. She tells me how she helped them and loaned them money which they never paid back. She's going on and on about how the world is a dark, dark place. I clear my throat: "Boy, Mrs. Leonardo, you've got a lot of stuff up here. Are you sure you want to keep it all?"

This is the wrong thing to say. Mrs. Leonardo's gray eyes get spitting mad and she says, *well,* she's seventy-six years old and she's had a *very* interesting life and she doesn't want to throw out anything of value. I look in a box with IRS tax forms dating back to 1955.

"Mrs. Leonardo, the IRS says you only need to keep tax records from the last three years. We could dump this whole box . . ." My mother told me this.

She lunges as much as a seventy-six-year-old person can and says she isn't giving her tax records to anyone so they can steal her secrets. Like tons of thieves are out there ready to pounce on this.

But at twenty-five dollars per hour, you learn to be patient. "Think of the money," my mother always says, "and the graciousness will come." So I'm taping the box and writing IMPORTANT PAPERS 1955–1963. Maybe she could turn this attic into a museum and people could walk through and learn all the things you should never hold on to.

Benjamin would have cracked under this pressure. Mrs. Leonardo is kneeling by a huge trunk, saying how the younger generation (mine) doesn't understand about manners, propriety, or simple human decency. Her grandniece, Veronica, walks around half naked with her belly button showing. She pulls old clothes out of the trunk and yanks this old lace tablecloth out and just looks at it. Finally, she says she got it when she was married and she's only used it once. She waited for a special occasion and only one came—her twentieth anniversary. No other occasion was special enough, and then her husband died right before their twenty-fifth anniversary and the tablecloth has been in this trunk ever since—only used once, she keeps saying—beautiful Egyptian linen. She looks kind of sad, though stiff. I say, "You could start using it now, Mrs. Leonardo," which is the wrong thing to say. She shuts that trunk and asks me just who do I think she's going to invite to dinner since everyone she's ever done anything for has either deserted her or died.

I don't know how to answer a question like this. My mother didn't cover it during Clean Sweep boot camp training where I learned how to scour a bathtub that a toddler spilled ink in, how to clean pet pee from any carpet known to man, how to wash windows and not leave streaks, how to open a refrigerator with year-old meat and not gag in front of the client. I pledged that the customer was always right and I, the lowly dust eliminator, was always, always wrong.

But I'm not sure what to do. If I agree with her, I'm not helping, and if I listen, I won't get the job done. The truth is, I don't like Mrs. Leonardo—so there's a big part of me that doesn't care—even though I know this is probably inhumane because she's a sad person, really. Kneeling there in the dust, surrounded by the boxes of her so-called interesting life, going on and on about people who are gone. I'm thinking about the next stage of the job—the actual cleaning of the attic which is going to take two people, and I know Benjamin will be hurled into monumental physical aberrations up here.

I'm tired, too, and my paper is late on King Lear who, in my opinion, thought too much and couldn't deliver. I'm thinking about my personal life—yes, dust eliminators have them. We have feelings; we have needs, dreams. I'm feeling that I work too much and I wish my mom had another business because what I do all day at school is exhausting enough without having to do heavy lifting after school and on the weekends. I think about when my dad died four years ago, and because of disorganization—that is, getting behind on paying his life insurance premiums—his insurance policy was cancelled and we got no insurance money when he died. He never meant to hurt us, but it was so scary not knowing if we could keep the house mixed with all the pain of losing him. We never got a regular time of mourning because we were fighting to stay afloat. Mom was trying to sort through Dad's huge piles of papers. We loved him so much, but he could never get rid of what Mom called his "clutter demons."

It took several months, but we got his papers sorted. We learned firsthand how you get organized, clean up, and obliterate dust. We became total aces at it; learned how widespread the problem truly is. We knew then we needed to share what we'd learned with others who were suffering, and felt that twenty-five dollars an hour was reasonable.

I'm not sure if Mrs. Leonardo wants someone to help or someone to complain to. Between you and me, I feel that listening to complaining *and* busting dust should earn thirty-five dollars per hour. But, I'm remembering being in our attic after my dad died; trying to go through his things. He had a trunk that his grandfather had given him—inside were all his photos and papers from school. I remember reading some of his essays from high school and just crying. I couldn't throw those out. Mom said going through all that was therapeutic for me because it was like being with him, kind of. He was forty-one years old when he died. Had a heart attack at work and was dead by the time the ambulance came.

Just thinking about the day makes me shaky. Over the years I've dissected every last thing I remember about the last morning I saw him. I should have made him breakfast—I knew how much he liked it when I did. I should have hugged him when he went out the door, but I was on the phone with Roger Rugsby who was my biology partner who needed me to go over my lab notes or he would fail. I missed the bus and Dad missed his train and he took me to school. I was late, so I hurled myself out of the car and he said, "Go get 'em, kiddo." That's the last thing he ever said to me. But I did better than Benjamin who overslept and didn't even see Dad that morning.

Mrs. Leonardo leans over a trunk like the one my father had. I want to say something encouraging to her, like, "Gee, Mrs. Leonardo, I know how hard it must be going through all these memories," or, "I hope sorting through all this is helping you the way it helped me." Memories are the only things we have left sometimes. You can hold a photo of a person you loved who's gone, but it isn't alive. Memories— the best ones—are filled with sights, smells, love, and happiness. I try to hold some of those in my heart for my dad each day.

She goes through the trunk, stony-faced. I can't tell what she's found, can't tell if she's going to torch the contents or hold them to her heart. I lug a big bag over and throw old newspapers inside. Mrs. Leonardo stops going through the trunk. She's holding something in her hands, not moving. I look at her stiff face and for a moment in the weird light of the attic, she looks like she's going to cry. But that's impossible. Then I hear a sniff and she says softly, "My mother read this book to my sister and me every night before bed."

I look at the book—a well-worn brown leather cover. Doesn't look like much.

"I thought she had it," Mrs. Leonardo says sadly.

"Who had it?"

"My sister, Helen. I thought she had the book. She always wanted it."

In these situations it's best to say, "Oh."

"I thought . . . I thought I'd sent it to her after Mother died." She looks down.

I say, "It's hard to remember what you've done after someone important dies."

"But, she'd asked me for it. It was the one thing she'd wanted."

"Well . . ."

"I haven't talked to her since Mother died. I thought she . . ."

I'm not sure how to ask this. Is Helen still alive?

I dance around it. "What do you think you should do with the book, Mrs. Leonardo?" She doesn't answer.

I try again. "Why did Helen want it so bad?"

She hands me the book. "She said these stories were her best memories of childhood." I look through it. "The Naughty Frog," "The Little Lost Tulip," "Spanky, the Black Sheep." It's amazing what we put up with as children. But then I remember my favorite bedtime story—"Rupert, the Church Mouse"—about this little mouse who lives in a church and polishes all the stained glass windows every night before he goes to sleep so the light can come forth every morning.

"I know she lives in Vermont," Mrs. Leonardo offers. "I heard from a cousin a while ago . . ." Her voice trails off.

"I think you should call her, Mrs. Leonardo."

She shakes her old head. No—she couldn't possibly.

"I think you should call her and tell her you've got the book."

She glares at me. "I believe we're done for today." She grabs the book from my hands, puts it back in the trunk.

"Sorry, ma'am. I didn't mean . . ."

She heads down the attic stairs.

I tell Benjamin that I don't want to hear about his problems, that his back looks strong to me, the shooting pain in his leg will go away eventually, and his headache is just a reflection of his deep, inner turmoil. I say this as we're walking to Mrs. Leonardo's house.

"I think my whole left side is going numb," he whispers pitifully as we walk up her steps.

"Deal with it."

Mrs. Leonardo is waiting for us. We're late. I don't mention that having to drag a hypochondriac four doors down the street takes time. Great food smells swirl from her kitchen.

Mrs. Leonardo looks Benjamin up and down, not impressed. "You've not been here before," she says. Benjamin half smiles and rubs his tennis elbow, which makes me nuts because he doesn't play tennis.

I introduce them. Tell her Benjamin is here to help with dust elimination and heavy lifting, at which point Benjamin leans painfully against the wall and closes his eyes.

"He's a very dedicated worker once he gets started, Mrs. Leonardo."

I jam my elbow into his side.

Okay, so we're cleaning this cavernous attic like there's no tomorrow. We've got all the trunks and boxes wiped down and pushed to the far side. We're running the turbo-charged

Clean Sweep Frankenstein portable vacuum that is so power-ful it can suck up pets and small children if they get too close. Benjamin is wearing a dust mask over his nose and mouth—he wrote *The Terminator* over it. This boy is appropriately miser-able, pulling down spiders' webs, sucking up dust mites. I can almost hear their little screams of terror. Almost, but not quite. My mother claims she can hear dust mites shrieking for mercy and uses this in her presentation if she thinks potential clients can handle it.

"Get the lace tablecloth from the trunk!" Mrs. Leonardo shouts from downstairs.

What's she want with that?

"And bring the book, too," she hollers impatiently.

I don't mention that we've shoved everything in the cor-ner like she said to, that I'll have to move it all to get to the trunk, and, by the way, I'm going as fast as I can. I get the book and the lace tablecloth that's been folded in very old plastic. I look at the book—reddish brown leather—*Aunt Goody's Good Night Stories*, it's called. Benjamin comes over looking like some kind of cosmic alien with his mask, takes the book, starts laughing.

"The Naughty Little Frog," he says reading. "Once upon a time there was a naughty little frog named Edmond. Edmond was so naughty that he never, ever cleaned his lily pad. It got so dirty that his mother had to make him stay on that lily pad several times each day to—"

"You're going to have to wait for the end." I yank the book from his hands and head down the creaky attic stairs with the tablecloth. Mrs. Leonardo is in the kitchen wearing a frilly apron, stirring a pot of something that smells beyond great.

She turns to look at me, puts her wooden spoon down.

"Help me put it on the table," she orders.

I'm smiling a little now because I know this tablecloth's history. I'm wondering who's coming to dinner.

"Looks like you're having a party," I offer as we get the tablecloth squared perfectly on the table.

Mrs. Leonardo says nothing, sets the table for two with what looks like the good silverware, the good napkins. Then she puts the storybook in front of one of the place settings.

"My sister, you see . . ." She pauses emotionally. "Well, she's . . . coming to dinner."

"You mean the one you haven't seen for a long time?"

"I only have *one* sister."

I'm just grinning now and I tell her I hope they have the best dinner in the world.

"Well, I do too." She looks nervously out the window and says whatever work we haven't finished can be done tomorrow. "You were right about . . . calling her, Katie."

I smile brightly, wondering if she's going to offer me some of her great-smelling food to show her gratitude. She doesn't. I head up the attic stairs and drag Benjamin to safety. He's sneezing like he's going to die. I take off his Terminator dust mask and lean him against a wall. Half of me wants to give Mrs. Leonardo a little hug of encouragement, but the other half warns, *Don't touch clients because they can turn on you.*

"Whatever you're cooking, Mrs. Leonardo, it sure smells good," I shout. "Your sister's going to love it." I'm not sure she hears all of that. Benjamin is into his fifth sneezing attack.

She nods from the kitchen; I push Benjamin out on the street.

"I could have died up there," he shouts, blowing his nose. "But you didn't."

And I remember the book my dad would read to us when we were little about the baby animals and their parents and how each mother and father animal kissed their babies good night. That book was chewed to death, ripped, stained, and missing the last two pages, but I wouldn't give it up for anything.

We walk back home almost silently, except for Benjamin's sniffs, sneezes, and groans. People just don't understand what important things can be hiding in the dust.

Mom says that all the time in her presentation.

ABOUT THE CONTRIBUTORS

M. T. ANDERSON lives in Boston, Massachusetts. He has published three novels for teens—*Thirsty, Burger Wuss,* and *Feed*—as well as work for adults and for younger children. He teaches writing at Vermont College.

> *The only way I can remember what happened to me as a kid is by remembering what book I was reading at the time. By reading books and writing, I explored what it meant to be other people. Or maybe what it meant to be me. And how to lie to tell the truth. And how to reveal things by concealing them, or maybe how to conceal things by revealing them. It was confusing, but the only thing on TV was* Starsky and Hutch.

• • •

JOAN BAUER, author of Newbery Honor and Christopher Award winner, *Hope Was Here*, has written numerous books for young people, including *Rules of the Road* (winner of the *Los Angeles Times Book Prize*), *Backwater* (A Smithsonian Best Book), *Squashed* (winner of the Delacorte Press Prize for a First Young Adult Novel), *Sticks*, and most recently, *Stand Tall*. She lives with her family in Brooklyn, New York.

> *Why do I read?*
>
> *I just can't help myself.*
>
> *I read to learn and to grow, to laugh and to be motivated. I read to understand things I've never been exposed to. I read when I'm crabby, when I've just said monumentally dumb things to the people I love; I read for strength to help me when I feel broken, discouraged, and afraid. I read when I'm angry at the whole world. I read when everything is going right. I read to find hope. I read because I'm made up not just of skin and bones, of sights, feelings, and a deep need for chocolate, but I'm also made up of words. Words describe my thoughts and what's hidden in my heart. Words are alive—when I've found a story that I love, I read it again and again, like playing a favorite song over and over. Reading isn't passive—I enter the story with the characters, breathe their air, feel their frustration, scream at them to stop when they're about to do something stupid, cry with them, laugh with them.*

Reading, for me, is spending time with a friend.
A book is a friend.
You can never have too many.

• • •

MARION DANE BAUER is the author of more than thirty books for young people. She has won numerous awards, including a Newbery Honor for her novel *On My Honor* and the Kerlan Award from the University of Minnesota for the body of her work. She is a writing teacher as well as a writer and she is former faculty chair and continues on the faculty at Vermont College for the Master of Fine Arts in Writing for Children and Young Adults program. Her books have been translated into more than a dozen different languages, and her nonfiction book, the American Library Association Notable Book for Children *What's Your Story?: A Young Person's Guide to Writing Fiction,* is used by writers of all ages. Marion Dane Bauer lives in Eden Prairie, Minnesota.

The tattered blue book entitled Stories That Never Grow Old *referred to in "The Good Deed" came into the story directly from my own bookshelf. And it came to my present bookshelf directly from my childhood. It was a gift from a beloved aunt the Christmas I was two, one I treasured throughout my childhood and treasure still. Every time I opened the blue covers,* The Little Engine That Could *chuffed heroically up the mountain, Mr. Fox tricked the young brown bear into losing his tail in the ice, the ugly duckling discovered that he was actually a beautiful swan. Each story made my world larger, and each reading made my world safe with its predictable repetition. But most important of all, this book and others by their many different authors put me in touch with the deepest, most creative thoughts of other human beings. They helped me to know what is possible. They helped me to know myself!*

• • •

ELLEN CONFORD wanted to be a writer from the time she made up poems from her spelling words in third grade. Since 1971 she has written more than fifty books for children. She lives in Great Neck, New York, with her husband, a college professor. She has one son, a musician.

I got my first library card when I was seven years old. The day I got it, I took eight books out of the library. I read them all, and went back the next week for eight more. I did that every week as long as I was in school. And I still do. Reading is one habit that I never want to give up.

• • •

MARGARET PETERSON HADDIX is the best-selling author of many books for children and teens. Her books for young readers include *Running Out of Time; Among the Hidden; Among the Impostors; Among the Betrayed; Don't You Dare Read This, Mrs. Dunphrey;* and *Just Ella.* Her work has been honored with the International Reading Association Children's Book Award,

American Library Association Best Books for Young Adults and Quick Pick for Reluctant Young Adult Readers citations, and several state reader choice awards. Margaret Peterson Haddix lives with her family in Columbus, Ohio.

> *I worked as a literacy tutor for adults for a while; now that my kids are in elementary school I volunteer in their classrooms, often working with kids struggling to learn to read. I have always been impressed with how hard the students try—sounding out words, puzzling over the nonphonetic spellings of the English language. And I am often saddened by what a painful ordeal reading becomes for them. I sometimes wish I could fast-forward their skills so they could see what they are working toward: not just competence, the ability to read signs on the highway, but the joy of reading, the delight of losing themselves in a story that becomes, somehow, all their own. "Escape" is based loosely on stories a bookstore owner once told me about all the women who came into her store to buy books for their husbands and boyfriends in prison. I felt so sorry for those women. But I was also delighted to hear that even in prison—maybe especially in prison—books still have so much value and power.*

• • •

JENNIFER L. HOLM is the author of *Our Only May Amelia*, a Newbery Honor Book, and the Boston Jane series. Ms. Holm lives in Brooklyn, New York. She has no desire to ever live on Mars.

You know that feeling you get in the pit of your stomach when you reach the top of a roller coaster? How the whole world is spread out before you? The way you hang in midair, and then suddenly, without warning, the coaster starts moving, and you are flying around the curves, your breath held, your heart pounding, your eyes open a squint.

Well, that's the same feeling you get when you read a book. Because when you read, you can go anywhere—back to the Revolutionary War or straight ahead to the future—it's all there, just waiting for you to experience it.

So go ahead, pick up a book—and enjoy the ride!

• • •

KATHLEEN KARR was the recipient of the 2000 Golden Kite Award for Best Fiction for *The Boxer*. She has also received ALA Notable Books for Children and Best Books for Young Adults commendations for her historical fiction for young readers. Her titles include *The Great Turkey Walk, Man of the Family, Playing with Fire, Skullduggery,* and *Bone Dry*. She lives with her husband in Washington, D.C.

My children's only complaint about my books is "Mom, you keep trying to teach everybody how to read!" Well, yes, maybe I do. Reading is important to me. Education is important to me. Perhaps this is the result of being raised by a father who waited on tables to pay his way through college, and a mother who was dragged out of school entirely too young—kicking and screaming the whole way. Perhaps it's the result of growing up on a farm where reading was my chief entertainment. Words have always been necessary to me, and the best way to collect words is through reading. I try to give this gift to the world by writing books that kids want to read. Could there be a better goal?

• • •

ALEXANDRIA LaFAYE loves to hide away and write in "The Outback," the office attached to the back of her garage. She has written many novels, including *The Year of the Sawdust Man, Edith Shay,* and *Dad, in Spirit.* When she isn't writing or puttering around in her garden with her three cats, Ian, Simon, and Yezi, she's teaching children's literature, young adult literature, and creative writing at California State University. In the summers, she often teaches in the children's literature program at Hollins University. She lives in San Bernardino, California. Her most recent book is *The Strength of Saints.*

I began reading by pictures. I still remember my first reading of Where the Wild Things Are. *The pictures convinced me that Max was in danger in the land of the wild things. It was only through his excellent portrayal of a wild beast that he kept those wild things from eating him. When I learned to read words by sounding out the syllables in a tiny book called* Clip Clop, *I discovered the dual world of words and pictures. I had a rough time learning to read, but when I finally got good at it, there was no stopping me. Now I just wish I had the time to read all the books I long to read.*

• • •

GREGORY MAGUIRE is the author of a dozen novels for children, including the popular series called The Hamlet Chronicles, as well as adult novels: *Wicked, Confessions of an Ugly Stepsister,* and *Lost.* He is a founder and codirector of Children's Literature New England, an advocacy group established in 1987. His most recent books for children are *The Good Liar* and a reissue of *The Dream Stealer.* He lives in Concord, Massachusetts.

If you wandered into the children's room of a public library—one of the older libraries, with high ceilings, and lots of wall space between the topmost shelves and the molding— you might find several hundred posters about reading. Printed over the decades by various limbs of the American Library Association, the posters show hundreds of kids in hundreds of positions of reading. Kids flying on books like kites, kids climbing on mountains of books, kids opening windows made of book covers, kids with books as wings. I only remember one motto: BOOKS FALL OPEN, YOU FALL IN. I always think it's nice of libraries to hang up some posters, but it's a bit of what they call preaching to the choir. If you've wandered into a library, you already believe. You already know it. Still, I like the posters, too. They're right, in all their fanciful acrobatics. BOOKS FALL OPEN, YOU FALL IN. When you climb out again, you're a bit larger than you used to be.

• • •

ELLEN WITTLINGER writes novels for young adults. Her books have won a number of awards, including a Michael L. Printz Honor, the Lambda Literary Award, and several ALA Best Book Awards. Her latest book is *The Long Night of Leo and Bree*. She lives in Massachusetts.

I doubt there are many writers who weren't avid readers during their childhoods. I classify myself among them, but my choice of literature wasn't always of the highest quality. I think there was a whole year in which I digested little other than Marvel Comics. But eventually I moved on from comic books to mysteries, and from mysteries to the plays of Tennessee Williams and Eugene O'Neill. I remember stumbling upon these odd books in a deserted library aisle. I'd never read a play before, though I'd seen a few raucous musicals at the Muny Opera in St. Louis. But these books were different— these were important. The discovery of the importance of words is one I wish for every child. Words to hear of the experiences of other people, and perhaps eventually, words to write of their own experiences.

I came from a family where reading was regarded as a rather frivolous entertainment that got in the way of "real" work. But I believe, had I not been a reader, the possibilities for my life would have been limited. Books were the window through which I glimpsed a larger world, and, eventually, the door through which I entered it.